Fiction Favours the Facts - Book 2

Mark Morgan

Bible
Tales
www.BibleTales.online

Published in Australia by Bible Tales Online.
www.BibleTales.online

Fiction Favours the Facts – Book 2

ISBN (Paperback) 978-1-925587-22-7
ISBN (eBook): 978-1-925587-23-4

Cover pictures of herons by Philip Morgan.

Picture of Hosea and Gomer on back cover is Copyright Arabs for Christ. See Acknowledgements and Thanks for details.

Free Download

Paul in Snippets

An 81-page PDF novelette by Mark Morgan.

The life of Paul painted from the Acts of the Apostles.

Get your free copy of *Paul in Snippets* when you sign up for the Bible Tales mailing list. As well as the eBook, you will receive a weekly email newsletter with micro tales, informative articles and special offers.

Visit **http://www.BibleTales.online/free-pins**

www.BibleTales.online

To my ever-patient wife Ruth.

Contents

Introduction

This book contains a collection of micro-tales that were first published in every second issue of the weekly Bible Tales newsletter between 25 August 2017 and 5 November 2018.

You may ask: Micro-tales? What are they?

Quite simply, they are short stories about Bible characters or events. Some are about Bible characters you may never have heard of, while others concentrate on an incident in the life of one of the more famous Bible characters.

BibleTales Online produces Bible-based fiction – the facts of the Bible rounded out with imaginative detail to help readers participate in the lives and feelings of real people.

I hope you enjoy this collection.

Mark Morgan
www.BibleTales.online
March 2019

Acknowledgements and thanks

Particular thanks go to Ruth, my wife, who helped me find time to write, patiently read what I wrote, and humoured me when I spent inordinate amounts of time on research into minute details.

Cathy, my oldest daughter, has tirelessly undertaken the thankless task of copy editing and proof reading each of the stories before they were published in the newsletter, and has also reviewed the entire manuscript. Thanks, Cathy.

Thanks to Philip, my youngest son, who drew the two pictures of herons used on the cover.

Feedback from a few newsletter subscribers has also improved the stories, so I thank them.

Almost all of the pictures come from the vast collection of illustrated Bible stories hosted by FreeBibleimages.org. All of the original illustrations used are copyright Sweet Publishing with the exception of the picture of Hosea (http://freebibleimages.org/illustrations /hosea/ Slide 2 – also used on the back cover) which is copyright Arabs for Christ. The digitally adjusted compilations from which they are taken are copyright FreeBibleimages. No alterations have been made to any of these illustrations and they are made available under a Creative Commons Attribution-ShareAlike 3.0 Unported license (see https://creativecommons.org/licenses/by-sa/3.0/).

Six public domain pictures from openclipart (www.openclipart.org) are used in the stories. These are acknowledged where they are used.

A request

If you find any errors, dear reader; typos, spelling errors, poor grammar, unkempt use of vocabulary, or, most importantly, errors of fact where the story misrepresents the Bible, please let me know. I can't correct printed books, but electronic versions and any new printed editions can be fixed.

Part One: Old Testament

One

Laban's Lament

For the true story, see Genesis 29-31.

It's just not fair.

How come Jacob has ended up with everything he wanted and I get nothing? Everything that he has was mine and, to be frank, it still should be.

My name is Laban. I live in Paddan-aram, north-east of Canaan, and Jacob is my son-in-law. I had two beautiful daughters, but they have been stolen from me. I had enormous flocks of sheep and goats, but they too have been stolen. Even my chief shepherd – an excellent worker, as I have always said – has gone.

It's quite a long story, but I think it is worth telling the whole sorry tale so that you will see clearly how badly I have been treated.

About 20 years ago, my nephew Jacob had to run away from home because of some trouble with his brother Esau. He came to me because he knew that I would look after him – and he had probably heard about my daughters, too.

Naturally, I welcomed him into my home and he

stayed for a month as I helped him get acquainted with the area, lending a hand with my sheep and things like that.

It didn't take long to see that he was head over heels in love with my younger daughter, Rachel. I could have used that attachment to make him my slave forever, but that's not my way. I believe in fairness. At least, I did. Now, I'm not so sure.

Anyway, after that first month, I was upfront with him and said that he didn't have to serve me for nothing just because he was my kinsman, and I pressed him to name his wages. Of course, having watched him looking at Rachel, I had my suspicions what he would want, so I had been dropping hints all month about the going rate for bride prices around here. I'm afraid I may have exaggerated the price a little, and I was almost embarrassed when he offered to work for seven years to be able to marry Rachel. Seven years! – I would have been very happy with three, but he had made the offer, so I didn't want to argue. We agreed on the deal and he kept working for me.

Jacob was a very good worker and an excellent shepherd. My flocks and herds were expanding at an enormous rate and I couldn't have been happier – except that the seven years were flying by and Leah still wasn't married.

I truly did all I could to find a suitable young man for her, or even an old one if necessary, one who was willing to pay the amount I needed. Jacob had set a high expectation for bride prices, and none of Leah's potential suitors were willing to pay so much for her. She was a very attractive girl in her own way, but those eyes did tend to put people off, particularly when they heard that I was expecting the equivalent of seven or eight years' wages to win her hand in marriage.

As everyone knows, the older sister had to be married before the younger one, so things began to get a little tense as the years passed. Of course, I couldn't talk to Jacob about it – it would have been too embarrassing for him. So I just let things go. After about six years, there was a little nibble from a rich old man – he was even older than me – who wanted a young wife, but unfortunately he lost his courage when I suggested a starting price of 10 years' wages. Maybe I was a little greedy there, but I still think she was worth every penny of it. I would have been willing to negotiate.

Nevertheless, it made me hope, and that distracted me so that I didn't talk to Jacob about the situation. I wanted to explain fully what would happen if Leah was not married when the seven years were up, but I never got around to it.

When the day arrived, I had no choice. Wanting to make sure that Leah and Rachel didn't get too badly upset or make a scene, I hadn't told them what was happening. In the morning, I sent Rachel away to see a distant relative. For some reason, she seemed almost distraught. Anyway, once she had gone, I told Leah the news, and she seemed upset too, but when I made it clear that there was no choice, she toned down the crying a little. I've no doubt she saw the necessity of it eventually. Some of us have to make difficult decisions at times, and those around us often don't appreciate the heavy burden it places on us. I don't mind doing it, but I do think it deserves a little acknowledgement.

Anyway, the day was a wonderful success, with all the local people crowded around to celebrate. Feasting and drinking all day, while Jacob constantly looked around for the bride and asked me from time to time when she was coming. I told him that it was common practice in Paddan-aram for the bride not to make an appearance until just before the formal part – the actual wedding ceremony that would make them man and wife. I have been to a wedding like that, too.

Jacob served Laban seven years to marry Rachel, but when the seven years were finished, Laban gave him Leah instead[1]

By the time it got dark that night, Jacob was getting rather impatient, and he was very eager to go over and greet Leah when I introduced her to the crowd. I made a bit of a joke out of it as I told him that he would need to stand on the other side of the marquee until the ceremony was over. We got on with the ceremony straight away. Jacob didn't even seem to notice that, behind the veil, it was Leah he was marrying, and I had made sure that there were no names mentioned in the promises they made to

[1] http://freebibleimages.org/illustrations/jacob-wedding/ Slide 9 (Sweet Publishing / FreeBibleImages.org, CC BY-SA 3.0 Unported)

each other. I suppose the lamps weren't very bright, but you would think a man would notice whom he was marrying!

Then, the next morning he came storming up to me as if the world had just come to an end. Now I was perfectly ready to give a little explanation, just to clarify the situation, but Jacob acted as if he hadn't known that I couldn't possibly give away the younger daughter before the older one. He got quite unreasonably angry as I explained to him that he was, of course, welcome to marry Rachel as well, but naturally, Leah had to be married first because she was older.

It took all of my skills as a negotiator to convince him that there was no real problem and that he wouldn't even have to wait for the full seven years before I gave him Rachel: I was willing to trust him and hand over Rachel as soon as Leah's bridal week was finished.

Despite my generosity in giving him Rachel early, I still sensed that he was not happy with me.

So, as you can see, I provided him with the two very best wives he could have found anywhere, and he stayed with me for fourteen years. By that time he had 11 sons, and you would have thought he would be very content with his lot in life. I would have been willing to let him stay indefinitely, but the very day that his 14 years were up, he came to talk to me about leaving.

Maybe I was too generous, but Jacob really is a good worker and El Shaddai his god seems to look after him too. There was no doubt that my flocks and herds had grown much larger and better under his care, so when he suggested that he could continue his work and receive as his wages all the sheep that were streaked, spotted and generally unattractive, that seemed like a fair deal. People want clean, creamy wool and goatskins that are a smooth, even black, so the ones he was asking for were less valuable anyway. Strange that he should ask for them, really. Nevertheless, when I did a quick head-count, I was surprised how many there were with those untidy markings.

As I walked through the flocks that afternoon, it occurred to me that then would be a good time to make some minor changes to the management of my flocks and herds. Since Jacob would be having a small holding of sheep and goats from that time on, some confusion of ownership might arise, so I decided to take one simple step to guarantee my sons' inheritance: that afternoon, I arranged for my sons to take those undesirable, low-value animals three days' journey away to avoid any possible confusion.

Once again, Jacob seemed to misunderstand or deliberately misconstrue my motives, and it was clear that he was angry when he examined the flocks the next day. It is quite hard to work with people when they are so moody.

Time passed and Jacob kept working – and the flocks kept growing amazingly. Lots of strong lambs and kids were being born, but the really unfair thing was the proportions of lambs with black on them and of goats with white patches. We had made an agreement, and under that agreement, he was getting all of those healthy young animals. I tweaked the conditions a few times to try to make sure that there was an equitable and sustainable division of the young, but whatever the settings were, those confounded ewes and nannies kept giving birth to animals with the wrong sorts of markings. Not only that, but it was always the strongest and healthiest mothers whose young had whatever markings Jacob was to benefit from.

It was clear that the gods were not doing what they should for me – and what I had a right to expect, given my consistent and generous provision of sacrifices to them.

Each year, Jacob's share of the flocks continued to grow. It really hurt to watch my hard-earned wealth slipping away.

It started to prey on my mind: all the benefits that Jacob was taking from me! He had taken both of my daughters, not just the one he had asked for. He had so many sons he made my family look small. And the gods were ganging up on me to give him my flocks. For the last six years I have had to fight to minimise my losses and avoid a complete takeover of my flocks.

Then came the crowning insult, the overwhelming offence: he not only ran away, but he also stole my gods! Yes, you read that right: he waited until I was away shearing the few sheep I had left and then packed up his family and hotfooted it for Canaan – taking my household gods with him.

The shearing took a while and Jacob had been gone three days before I returned and heard the news. Quickly, I took up the chase – those gods were valuable and theft shouldn't be left unpunished! I pursued them hard and then, just the night before I caught up with them, the God of Jacob's father, Isaac, spoke to me and told me not to say anything good or bad to Jacob.

Seven days of determined, anger-filled pursuit, and then I wasn't going to be able to take any positive action at all. I'm sure you can see why I am complaining: God keeps helping Jacob and picking on me.

The next day, I finally caught them and told Jacob just what I thought of him, while dutifully obeying God's limitations as far as I could. Then he had the gall to hide behind God's protection and blame my treatment of him for his foolish flight!

I'm not sure where they had hidden them, but I couldn't find my household gods. I don't have any doubt that someone took them – probably with Jacob's help. He might even have used one of my own daughters to do the dirty deed. It really isn't fair.

Two

Crime and Punishment

For the true story, see Genesis 33:18-35:7.

Dinah didn't make it home that night.

At first, everyone thought she was just a little late, then a lot late. Someone – no-one could quite remember who – suggested that maybe she had done a bit more than just visit the house of one of her friends.

Warning[2]

Nobody had any knowledge of anything like that, so one of the servants was dispatched to find her.

---

[2] "warning" by yves_guillou:

At first, they weren't really worried. Not really. Nothing could really go wrong with a young girl visiting her girl friends. Could it?

Still, she was late and something had to be done.

The servant returned with two companions – a young woman called Basemath and a girl, Judith, in her early teens – and a tale that took some time to unravel. He led them first to Leah, Dinah's mother.

It turned out that the young woman was actually the girl's mother, although she couldn't have been more than 25. The girl was one of Dinah's new friends. They both looked rather pleased, although the girl's attitude might have been tinged with jealousy. It was hard to understand. Both were eager to spill the news.

"Such news we have to tell you!" announced the mother. "You'll be so pleased."

"He's so handsome," breathed the daughter.

"She's made such a conquest! He's the son of Hamor, the prince, you know."

"Who are you talking about?" asked Jacob, who had arrived in time to hear the end of this gleeful statement.

"Why, Shechem, of course," said Basemath.

Jacob and Leah looked at each other; but both looked blank. "Can you start the story from the beginning?" asked Leah.

"You'll be so pleased," repeated Basemath.

"It was a bit underhanded, I think," said young Judith with a pout. "The sneaky little thing."

"But such a catch!" smiled Basemath. "And so masterful."

"You were going to explain," begged Leah. "Please start at the start."

"Oh, but surely you must know something about it? Dinah wouldn't have gone out with the rest of the girls if she hadn't been looking for love. That's why they went out today. Young girls, looking for young men to marry. Trying to catch the best one they can. That's how it works around here. That's how I got my husband, and I was about Dinah's age."

Jacob and Leah looked at each other again, and now they each saw concern in the other's eyes.

"Can you please explain what happened?" repeated Leah, desperately.

"Well, it's all very simple really," said Basemath, obviously disappointed and a little miffed that her good news had not been welcomed with the joy it deserved. "Dinah went out with Judith and her friends this afternoon. They did the ordinary sorts of things that girls do to attract a husband, and Shechem noticed Dinah joining in with the rest."

"He talked to her very nicely, all gentle and kind," said Judith, "but it was obvious from the start that he liked the look of her. They spent some time talking and then he asked her to come with him for a walk, just by themselves. Well, she said that she had better not, that you wouldn't want her to. I thought she was just being coy, so I took her aside and told her that it would be alright and that Shechem was a good catch. She said she really shouldn't, but I think she was weakening. In the end it was taken out of her hands anyway. I'm sure she liked the look of him – he's very handsome. But while we were talking, some of the other girls had been joking with Shechem, and one of them suggested that he should just pick her up and carry her off. And that's sort of what he did. He came over and told her straight out that he loved her. He was obviously serious. Then he leaned over and whispered in her ear. She looked pleased, but a little shocked, and then suddenly he swept her up in his arms and walked out."

Basemath was watching Leah's face and could tell that she was shocked by the news, so she hurriedly interrupted Judith, who looked as if she was about to go into more detail. "Anyway," she said, "Shechem is just wildly in love with your daughter, and I'm sure you will hear from his father very soon."

Judith was obviously a bit disappointed at this sudden truncation of her exciting story, and looked at her mother with irritation. But she took the chance to make one last contribution: "Apparently he carried her all the way to his room, up all of those stairs, too!"

Basemath hushed her daughter, and they left soon afterwards.

As soon as they had gone, Jacob and Leah discussed the news. Leah was distraught. Jacob was deeply upset too, but unsure about what to do.

"We don't know for sure what has happened," said Jacob, consolingly.

"Don't we?" sobbed Leah. "I don't think there's any doubt what has happened to Dinah."

"I suppose you're right, but we must go through and check. It is faintly possible that she hasn't been harmed."

"Is it?" asked Leah, still crying. She shook her head and wiped her tears. "I suppose it isn't completely impossible, but it's close. Oh, Dinah, Dinah, my dear little girl."

"They mentioned that this Shechem was a son of Hamor the prince, didn't they?"

"Yes," said Leah, dully.

"I suppose it must be the same Hamor from whom I bought this very piece of land that we are camping on," he mused. "What can we do to minimise the damage? I don't think we will be able to make his son suffer as I would dearly love to. Does this young prince think he can just grab any young girl who takes his fancy and carry her off? And it seems that the girls think it's a good idea too. What a society!"

The discussion went on for a long time as the two parents gradually came to terms with the devastating news. Retribution was high on their agenda, but they knew that they were outnumbered by the people of the land, who saw nothing wrong with such behaviour. Besides, servants couldn't be relied on very much and the sons who might have helped were away in the country, looking after the flocks.

If only Dinah had stayed home and not made friends with girls who had different standards! But now it was too late. The damage was irreversible.

Nothing could be done that night. The city gates would be closed and would not be opened for anyone.

The long slow hours of uncertainty until the morning must be endured.

But still, it was conceivable that the story had not followed the path that seemed inevitable. It was possible, faintly possible…

Early the next morning, even that faint possibility was taken away.

News, particularly news like that, travels quickly – sometimes almost unbelievably quickly. The sons of Jacob came in with the flocks shortly after dawn. They had heard the news and were seething with anger over their sister's treatment.

Jacob spent some time trying to calm them down a little. Some of them, Simeon and Levi in particular, were eager to attack the city as soon as the gates opened and kill everybody there. But Jacob felt that a little more caution was required, although he was pleased to see their fury at such an outrageous piece of presumptuous immorality.

Hamor and Shechem came to visit as soon as the city gates opened, by which time Jacob had calmed his sons down a little. However, their anger had not gone; instead, it had become a coldly calculating fury that would not rest until the wrongdoing had been punished. In fact, Simeon and Levi had still seemed so angry that Jacob had sent them away to do a small job together to take their minds off their rage.

Hamor came in and greeted them all happily, eager to have them agree to his plan to give their daughter to his besotted son and become fully integrated into the local community. Daughters could be swapped as wives and open trade enjoyed by all. Shechem didn't contribute much to the conversation, except to say that he was willing to give any bride price to get Dinah as his wife.

Of course, Hamor and Shechem hadn't brought Dinah with them – she had been left in the city. Bargaining chips are valuable and possession is power.

Together, Jacob and his sons spoke politely to Hamor, discussing his proposals for friendship and cooperation, without sounding eager, but without showing the fury they felt.

It was then that Simeon and Levi returned to join the conversation. They had used their time to great purpose, but not at all the purpose Jacob had intended. They had a plan.

Jacob explained to them the proposals and was surprised when they readily agreed with the suggestions, with just one proviso: all the men of the city must be circumcised. They spoke convincingly about the advantages to everyone of this course of action, and in the end it was agreed on as the way forward.

Hamor and Shechem left to convince their fellow citizens that having Jacob and his family join the community would be worth the discomfort of circumcision. Apparently, they were successful: the family heard the news – and the complaints about the pain – before the end of the day.

Then, two days later, Simeon and Levi put the main component of their plan into effect. Armed with swords and accompanied by some servants, they went into the city and killed Shechem, Hamor and all of the other men in the city. The pair were pleased with the outcome: Dinah had been rescued and punishment had been meted out. Shechem had humbled her and nothing could remove that, but Simeon and Levi were content that his immoral behaviour had earned its just reward.

Jacob was not pleased and spoke sternly to Simeon and Levi, but only about the danger in which the whole family had been placed by their actions. The surrounding villages, towns and cities, he said, could easily join together and attack the family.

His sons were not very concerned. They viewed their actions as necessary: should a man be allowed to treat their sister as a prostitute? Jacob understood their attitude, but he was seriously worried.

And what of Jacob's God? What was his response to these events?

God instructed Jacob to go to Bethel, and Jacob obeyed quickly. As they travelled, God sent a fear of the family on all of the surrounding people so that no one would make any attempt to attack them as they passed through.

Three

Up we go

For the true story, see 1 Samuel 14:1-46.

My hero was almost executed today for winning a battle.

I know that sounds pretty ridiculous, and I also know that the king would say it had nothing to do with winning the battle, but that's sure how it looked to me.

I am Prince Jonathan's armour bearer and he is my hero. I have always said that I would do anything that he asked me to do, and I think that today proved it.

Calculated risks are all very well, but this was just blind faith. Nevertheless, we came out of it alive and the Philistines didn't, so blind faith isn't always blind.

Prince Jonathan's father is King Saul, the first king of Israel, and he is a brave man – but not as brave as my master, Prince Jonathan.

This morning, our army and the Philistine army were just sitting around waiting for something to happen, but the prince had the idea of making it happen, instead of just waiting.

So he said to me, "Let's go over to the Philistine garrison on the other side." Of course, I agreed, and we sidled nonchalantly out of the camp, not letting anyone know we were going – particularly not the king! We made it out of the camp without being noticed and walked along a deep valley that led towards the army of the Philistines. They were spread out on a sort of plateau near the towns of Michmash and Geba, while we were down in the valley, a long way below them, at the bottom of some pretty steep cliffs. They had a couple of outposts keeping watch over the pass we were walking along, and the prince could see that we wouldn't be able to get past them without being spotted.

We paused out of sight of these outposts and talked about what we should do. "Come on, let's go over to the garrison of these uncircumcised," said Prince Jonathan. "It may be that the Lord will work for us, for nothing can hinder the Lord from saving by many or by few."

Well, that's one of the things I love about the prince: he has amazing faith in Yahweh our God. I have faith in God too, but not as much as the prince has. Instead, I have faith in Prince Jonathan. He decides what we two should do, based on his faith in God; and I do whatever the prince tells me because I have faith in his faith. It works pretty well.

The prince suggested that we show ourselves to the Philistines and do a little test. If they told us to come up to them when they saw us, then we would take that as a sign to go up because God would give them into our hand – although I wasn't really sure what that would look like. What can two men do against an army? Nevertheless, we went.

When the Philistine watchmen saw us, they immediately started laughing at us, saying that the Hebrews were crawling out of their holes. I suppose it was sort of true – we had been hiding in a big cave, and I think that was part of why Prince Jonathan wasn't happy. He didn't think that God's people should be hiding in holes like rats!

Then they told us to come up to them, promising that they would "show us a thing or two" if we did.

Jonathan and I looked at each other and he smiled at me with a confident, "There, what did you expect?" look in his eyes. I grinned back at him and we kept walking. When we reached the bottom of the cliff, Jonathan said, "Come up after me."

I didn't get upset when he said this because I know the prince too well, but I did remind him once again that he was forgetting what an armour-bearer is for: I am meant to go in front of him and protect him. But he wouldn't allow it. It was his choice, he said, for us to go and do such an impossible thing, so he had to lead. I can't imagine King Saul ever saying that to his armour bearer! What a wonderful king Prince Jonathan will make when the time comes.

Anyway, we climbed up, needing to use our hands as well as our feet – no chance of holding any weapons to defend ourselves. Throughout our climb, the Philistines could easily have used their spears or arrows to put an end to us, or even dropped stones on us. But they didn't.

Being in front, the prince reached the top first, and was up and at them before I had even made it up onto level ground. All I could do was to try and catch up.

By then the Philistines weren't laughing anymore.

A large crowd of them was waiting for us, but we didn't wait for them to greet us.

Prince Jonathan ran towards the crowd and hacked at the closest ones with his sword, injuring them and knocking them off balance, while I followed up behind him and finished them off one by one. It was hard work, because they all had good armour on, but we just kept moving straight through the crowd, and by the time we had killed about ten of them, I could see that the throng was thinning in front of us.

Sword and shield[3]

Then they started to run away, and we chased them. We killed about 20 men between us, and by then the rest were all fleeing, shouting and screaming.

I guess that they would eventually have regrouped, fought back and pushed us off the cliff if God hadn't chosen just that moment to send an earthquake.

Suddenly the earth was heaving and rolling, and the prince and I had to stop, just to stay on our feet.

---

[3] "Sword and shield icon" by purzen
(https://openclipart.org/detail/28731/sword-and-shield-icon)

Then, as I watched the fleeing Philistines, some of them fell over. Of course, the men running behind them didn't have time to stop, so they tripped over them and fell on top of them. And in the confusion and fear, they all thought it was us attacking them. Within moments, hundreds of Philistine warriors were fighting each other, and the shouting and panic continued to spread through the army.

It was then that the prince and I looked back towards our own camp and saw that there seemed to be a lot of movement there too. Within a very short time, Israelite soldiers were streaming towards the Philistine camp. There were still many more Philistines than Israelites, but the Philistines were all in a panic, too busy killing each other or running away to get organised to fight our army. Not only that, but every so often another earth tremor would shake the ground and terrify them all over again.

To cut a long story short, the Philistines ran in all directions, killing each other and never quite getting organised enough to fight back against our brave soldiers, who had been so badly outnumbered when they committed themselves to the attack. There were also lots of other Israelites hiding in the hills who saw what was happening and came out to attack the fleeing Philistines too. A wonderful victory was unfolding and the rout would have been complete, except that King Saul had made a pretty basic error. Of course, he wasn't trying to cause trouble, but his mistake almost killed my master.

You see, King Saul had given his soldiers an order that none of them should eat any food until night fell and they had finished defeating the enemy. But it wasn't just an order – he made it into a curse and an oath before Yahweh, so it was extra serious.

By the time we met up with some other Israelite soldiers in a forest, chasing Philistines together, there were hungry, worn out Israelites all over the countryside.

The prince and I had heard nothing of all of this, and as we entered the forest it seemed as if God was providing the special food that we needed. There were plenty of beehives around, and honey was dripping out onto the ground underneath. Prince Jonathan did the obvious thing: he used the staff in his hand to get some of the honey without disturbing the bees too much, then put it on his hand and ate it.

You should have seen the smile on his face and the way his eyes lit up. You'd appreciate some pure, delicious honey to fill you with instant energy too, if you had been doing all the hard work we had done that afternoon. I was about to follow his example when one of the men said to the prince, a hint of worry in his voice, "Your father strictly charged the people with an oath, saying, 'Cursed be the man who eats food this day.' "

Now you'll never hear Prince Jonathan criticising his father, even though the king isn't always very wise, because the prince always shows respect for his father, just as God commanded us. But this time he said that his father had caused trouble for the land, because the honey would have been just the thing to fill everyone with spirit for finishing off the battle.

Well, I didn't eat any of the honey because of the king's curse, but I didn't expect any trouble to come of the matter. When evening came, I found that I was wrong.

The curse expired at evening, and then there was quite a disturbance over food. Many of the men were so hungry that they were killing animals and eating them without properly draining out the blood. That got sorted out, but it seemed to put King Saul on his guard, as if he sensed that something was not quite right, and that Prince Jonathan had something to do with it. Maybe he was a bit jealous that his son had so bravely shown his faith in God and won an amazing battle.

Whatever the reason, King Saul asked God for an answer through Ahijah the priest, but God wouldn't answer. King Saul took that as a sign that someone had broken his curse. He asked everyone what had happened, but none of us would answer him. After all, no-one wanted to get Prince Jonathan into trouble after the amazing victory he had won!

But Saul could tell that we were hiding something, so he drew lots to find whether the problem was with his family or everyone else, and God said the fault was with King Saul and Prince Jonathan.

I was starting to get concerned by this time, but I felt that surely God wouldn't help Prince Jonathan to miraculously win a battle and then get him in trouble for breaking a rule he hadn't even known about. I should have known better, really, but I don't always understand God as well as I should.

God gave the answer alright, and the prince was very noble in offering to die if that was necessary. What a disaster that would have been! King Saul was ready to kill him, too, but everyone else stood up and said that it would be completely unjust, after the salvation the prince had achieved. Fortunately, we managed to convince King

Saul that it wasn't Prince Jonathan's fault, as he hadn't known.

We didn't try to show whose fault it really was, but I hope that the king learns not to take such foolish oaths and curses again!

So it is that we are all alive tonight, saved by the love of God and the courage and faith of Prince Jonathan. Not only that, but we are all happy because we helped to save the prince from his father's thoughtless curse.

I guess that the surviving Philistines are the ones who will be most unhappy tonight. Just this morning they were in a position of power, but now they have lost almost everything.

Four

Jericho Revisited

For the true story, see Joshua 6:26 and 1 Kings 16:34.

"Today we start a great work," shouted the leader, tall, dark and handsome. "This was once a mighty city, and we will restore it to the grandeur it deserves."

A large crowd of men surrounded him, men whose skin was burned dark by the sun and whose hands were rough from years of working with stone.

They stood together at the edge of a rugged piece of land. Uneven and blackened, its steep mounds and dark holes suggested the long-neglected rubble of a ruined city. No grandeur, just an untidy shambles of stones strewn hither and thither. Faint paths criss-crossing the waste suggested that many of the holes had animal inhabitants.

"Last week," continued the leader, "we did what we could to burn off the cover of bushes and trees. Now we can begin the real work of removing the old stones so that rebuilding can start."

Tall, dark and handsome Hiel of Bethel might be, but he was also determined, and the rebuilding of Jericho was his goal. In his mind, leaving Jericho as a pile of rubble was missing an important opportunity.

Many others had seen the opportunity, but had been overwhelmed by the local opposition to rebuilding. There were rumours, stories, undercurrents of horror that surrounded the place – at least, if one listened to the locals.

Hiel had swept all before him, overcoming the opposition of superstitious locals, as he viewed them, and even obtaining royal permission for the project. Jericho would be rebuilt and Hiel would have a special dispensation to collect taxes in the city for the king. When these taxes were collected, Hiel would pocket his share before the money went into the royal treasury.

And well would he deserve his share, for rebuilding a ruined city is no small task, and the costs were formidable. Already they were exceeding his initial estimates because of the timid reluctance of the locals. No-one would take on the work without receiving extra pay. Hiel had gritted his teeth and paid up.

Hiel continued: "We have set up stockpiles in four locations around the city. As you collect the stones, they are to be moved to the closest stockpile. Start on the outside perimeter and gradually move in to the centre. Any questions?"

No-one responded, so Hiel said, "If anyone has any problems, ask your supervisors. If they can't help, ask me, or if I am not here, ask my son, Abiram. Now, to work!"

It was hard work, but gradually the ordered piles of stones in the stockpiles grew and the rough hillocks became even ground. True, there were some nasty surprises with snakes and rats and other animals who objected to having their homes dismantled, but overall it wasn't too dangerous.

⚭

One day, Abiram asked his father, "How long has this city been ruined for?"

"About 500 years."

"How did it happen?" Abiram continued.

"The superstitious say that Yahweh made the walls fall down, but no-one really knows."

"And why has no-one rebuilt it before now? Hasn't anyone even tried?"

"No, no-one," said Hiel. "Everyone has been scared off by a superstition that there is a curse on the place." He laughed and then teased: "You'd better hope they're wrong, Abiram, because part of the curse involved the death of the oldest son of the one who rebuilt Jericho. But there you go, it's all just old wives' tales."

"Of course," agreed Abiram, laughing, but maybe a little unsure.

⚭

After several months, the wasteland of hillocks had finally been reduced to a clear, level surface on which the rebuilding of the city could begin in earnest.

Hiel was a careful planner, but also a bit of a showman.

The largest of the stones retrieved from the site had been set aside as the base for a large temple to be built in the middle of the city. As the clearing work neared completion, some of the men were put to work digging trenches in which the foundations of this first building in Jericho would be placed.

Hiel planned a big ceremony to which all the important people of the area and all the workers and their families would be invited to witness a special event, followed by a feast.

All day the preparations went on. Food was brought in carts and on the backs of donkeys; fire pits were readied and cooks prepared the food for cooking. Servants were instructed in their duties and the site was finally tidied. The four large foundation stones that were to be placed in the shallow trench during the ceremony were readied so that they could be lifted into their final positions while the guests looked on. A small platform had been built so that Hiel could direct the proceedings from its raised surface, admired by the crowd. At intervals through the day, he pictured the scene in his mind's eye and a satisfied smile crossed his handsome face. Already, he had achieved more with this site than anyone else had in 500 years.

Finally the time came; an enthusiastic crowd watched as Abiram supervised the placement of the stones while many men hung on the ropes to keep one of the massive stones in the air. Others slowly edged the arm of the derrick around to move the stone into the right place, just a short distance from the next stone. Abiram stood in the gap between the stones, making sure that there was just enough space to move between them. After a few small adjustments, the stone was in just the right position and ready to be lowered.

"Lower away," said Abiram, resting his hand on the stone so that he could guide it down into place. Maybe he felt the stone hit something, or maybe he just wanted to make sure the way was clear: whatever the reason, he knelt down between the stones to see under the stone that was now being quickly lowered into place.

"Wait..." he said. It was the last word he ever spoke. It all happened so quickly, as the other end of the stone landed on a large log that had been used to support the ends of the large stones earlier in the day when logs were being placed underneath as rollers. Inexplicably, no-one had noticed that it had been left in the very place this stone was to occupy, and now it supported the opposite end of the stone from where Abiram was bending as the lowering continued. With the log supporting one end and the rope lowering the other end, the stone suddenly began to tilt towards Abiram and there was nowhere for him to escape. In an instant, his head was crushed between the two massive stones and his life was snuffed out.

☙

There was no celebration that night. Hiel's oldest son was dead and all the ancient superstitions had been revived. The locals looked knowingly at one another and their whispered conversations always stopped as Hiel approached. It made him furious. Abiram's death had been a terrible accident – time and chance at its worst – but surely no-one could possibly link it to that old superstition?

Hiel sent away all of the men who had been involved in the operation. He could have had them punished or executed for their carelessness, but he was not a vindictive man.

Work on the city continued, a few civic buildings for the administration of the area and a massive wall surrounding the entire site. Over time, the whispered conversations ceased and Hiel was again able to enjoy the feeling of success that comes from a job well done.

His other three sons were working with him now, replacing Abiram, whose tragic death he still mourned every day. Even Segub, his youngest son, was working on the site, although Hiel's wife had strongly opposed that decision. But Segub had been eager to be involved and Hiel had felt justified in overriding his wife's excessive caution. Boys had to grow up some time.

Rebuilding[4]

Tall, thick walls now surrounded the rebuilt town. No more major accidents had taken place – it seemed as if the gods were blessing the work. Gatehouses presided over the newly constructed roads that led into the almost empty

---

[4] http://freebibleimages.org/illustrations/nehemiah-2/ Slide 1 (Sweet Publishing/FreeBibleimages.org, CC BY-SA 3.0 Unported)

city, and in only a few days the walls and gates would be complete and inhabitants could be brought into the newly secured city.

One by one, the large wooden gates were fitted into place and the bars that enabled them to be locked at night or in time of war were shaped and eased into place. These were massive pieces of wood, more like tree trunks than beams, able to withstand the fearsome blows of a battering ram should an army attack.

Finally, it was time to finish the work on the last gate. Hiel resisted the temptation to organise a special celebration. His wife had said that would be tempting fate – that there would be time enough for celebrations once the work was complete, new inhabitants were pouring into the city and their gold was pouring into Hiel's treasuries.

But he did allow himself a small party. He called all of his family together so that his sons and his wife could enjoy his success. He would have liked to remind her that her superstitious misgivings had been proven wrong, but he wanted her to decide that for herself. He had no time for superstitions.

They all gathered in the gatehouse where the men were making some final adjustments to the hinges on which the massive doors swung. And then it was time to fit the bars. Most of the work had already been done, but some final work with an adze was needed to make sure that the huge bulk of the bars would slide easily into the supports on the gate but without any extra free movement that would badly weaken the gates. Segub was really too young to help much, but he was popular with the men and they moved apart a little to make space for him as they placed and replaced the massive bar while the carpenter worked his skilful refinements.

A scrape here, a tap there, until the shavings lay around the gate and the men could put the bar in its slots with little effort. There was just one last small area that was still binding a little, so the men lifted the bar again as they had so many times. Possibly it was fatigue or maybe enough men slipped on the shavings at the same time that the weight became unbearable for the rest; whatever it was, suddenly the bar was falling as all the men jumped back. All except Segub. He slipped and fell to the cobblestones, and the massive timber bar fell across his shoulders.

CR

Jericho was rebuilt and filled with people once more. Hiel of Bethel was a household name admired by all. His coffers were filling nicely, too. But in his home and at his table there were two vacant places. Building Jericho had cost him dearly and still the locals whispered behind their hands about that old curse spoken by Joshua of old:

> "Cursed before the Lord be the man
> who rises up and rebuilds this city, Jericho.

> "At the cost of his firstborn shall he
> lay its foundation,
> and at the cost of his youngest son
> shall he set up its gates."

He had laid the foundation at the cost of his oldest son, Abiram – tall, dark and handsome like his father. Finishing the gates had cost him his youngest son Segub: but it was all just blind chance, wasn't it?

Wasn't it?

Five

Of Bears and Boys

For the true story, see 2 Kings 2:23-25.

Last year I learned a lesson that I will never forget. The scars on my right hand remind me of what happened every time I see them, and the hand still hurts a lot of the time, which makes me remember too.

But there is something else that brings the lesson to mind even more forcibly: the look that people give me when they meet me for the first time. The people of Bethel know me and are used to how my face looks, but Bethel is a popular place for visitors from all over Israel who come to worship the golden calf that Jeroboam the son of Nebat made. Visitors don't know me, and it's easy to recognise the horror on their faces when they catch sight of me for the first time.

I don't have to see my face, unless I look at the reflection in a still pool, and I haven't done that for months – nowadays I always make sure that I disturb the surface of the water before looking down. Feeling the shape of my face is bad enough; I still remember how my cheeks used to be smooth, and my forehead too. Now, I can trace the path of each of her claws, and I feel again the fear that raced through my veins as she stood up on her hind legs and swung her paw at me.

There was no time to dodge and no strength great enough to resist her. Those terrible claws raked across my forehead and down my face, and the blood immediately began to pour out. I screamed and put my hands to my face, trying to hold it together, and so it was my right hand that caught the force of her next blow. The weight of that blow threw me backwards and spun me around to fall face down in the dust of the road, where I lay, helpless, shaking with terror and unable to see anything because of the blood and dirt that filled my eyes. Lying there, I waited for her to continue her attack, waiting for the next hammer blow, the tearing, shredding impact of her claws. But nothing more came. My friends tell me that she ignored me and ran to attack another boy. For me, there was nothing but fear and blood and dust and pain.

Two blows; that was all. Just a few short moments of irresistible violence, but they changed my life forever.

It took months for me to recover my sight completely, and for months after that I wasn't sure that I really wanted to keep living. Constant pain and permanent disfigurement destroyed all optimism and life seemed bleak indeed.

But I was not the only one suffering.

Two bears and forty-two boys. Every one of us boys was injured by those bears, but I don't think anyone managed to hurt the bears in the slightest. Later, many hunters went out to search for them, but they found nothing, so no retribution was ever meted out.

Everybody in Bethel was talking about the event, and agreeing that it was a one in a million chance – two bears going completely crazy at the same time. All sorts of explanations were suggested: some said that the bears must have been defending their cubs; others suggested that the bears were fighting each other and we simply got in the way; and still others suggested that the bears must have been afraid that we were attacking them. The one thing that everyone agreed on was that it was not our fault, that it was just a freak accident and no-one was to blame.

But I know better.

It really was a major catastrophe for the town. Forty-two boys in the group, and every one of them was injured. Some less, some more – but all will wear scars for the rest of their lives. Some of the injured boys were brothers, but even so, there were still more than 30 families affected. If you count parents, siblings, grandparents and neighbours, it adds up to hundreds of people who were closely connected to at least one boy who was injured by those two bears.

The damage inflicted varied enormously. Some boys have only minor scars, although the pain and suffering were not minor at the time. But some only barely survived after spending weeks in bed when their wounds turned septic. I suppose it was quite amazing that none of us died.

But through it all, we were constantly fed the message, "It's not your fault". Yet we all knew that it wasn't true.

To get you to understand the facts, I need to tell you a bit more about what happened. The details are important and make all the difference between a random attack and a targeted punishment.

Just before harvest started that year, I and some of my friends had little to do in Bethel one afternoon, so we went out of the town and wandered down the road to look for some fun. We scrambled around on the rocks near the bottom of the hill, and took turns throwing stones at various targets.

Other young lads were doing the same that afternoon, and gradually we sort of coalesced into bigger and bigger groups until there were 42 of us in one big group, all sitting on the rocks near the road, talking and laughing.

At least, that's how it started.

Then some of the boys started making comments about the travellers who passed by. Quiet comments, trying to be clever. For example, one man with large ears was described as "donkey ears", but he didn't hear, and no-one got hurt.

I didn't get involved at first, because I don't really like that sort of thing: it's not showing the respect we should show to others. Nevertheless, the comments got gradually louder, and having 41 others there in support made us all so much braver. Then a man with a limp heard when my friend called him a cripple. It wasn't even a clever thing to say, but I didn't do anything to stop it. I just laughed with the rest of them while the man hurried past as quickly as he could, looking scared.

The harassment of passers-by quickly worsened, until every passing traveller was sneered and jeered at. If any of our parents had been present, we would have quickly felt the heavy hand of their disapproval, but we were unsupervised and out of control.

I wasn't happy, but I didn't do anything to stop it by word or action: just provided tacit support, and sometimes even joined in. I am very ashamed to admit it. Afraid to make a stand for good, I joined the crowd in evil. At least I could have left.

But I didn't.

After about an hour of this, a man of medium height walked up the road near us, heading towards the gates of Bethel.

He was strong and muscular – a man whom I wouldn't have dared to laugh at if I had been alone. His dark beard suggested that he was not particularly old, but despite that, he was bald. A small ruff of curly hair decorated the back of his head where it joined his neck, but apart from that, he was completely bald!

With a laugh, one boy said to his neighbour, as they sat together on a rock, "Look at him, he's as bald as a brick!"

"Baldy," called his friend, and it caught on.

"Go away, you bald-headed bed-knob," sneered another.

It spread until we were all joining in – yes, I'm ashamed to admit that I joined in too.

"Go away, you bald-head," I shouted.

The man had turned and looked at us when the verbal onslaught began, but he neither turned to flee nor came running at us brandishing the long staff he carried.

Instead, he stopped and stood still, clasping his staff in both hands and looking up at us.

We were working ourselves up into a frenzy of shouting, and I think we might even have run at him or started throwing stones if he hadn't suddenly held up a hand. It was an imperious gesture and we all instantly stopped shouting.

"You boys should show more respect to your elders and to Yahweh, the living God. He has sent me, Elisha, as a prophet to take the place of the great prophet Elijah, and now you are cursed in the name of Yahweh, the God of Israel."

That was all he said. Then he turned away and walked back down the road, back towards the main north-south road, as if he had decided he didn't want to go to a town that had people like us in it.

His words calmed us down all of a sudden, I can tell you. A prophet had cursed us! We sat for a few moments in silence, looking at each other uneasily and wondering what would happen as the figure of Elisha walked down the hill and disappeared around a corner.

Then the horror began.

Attacking bear[5]

---

[5] "attacking bear" by johnny_automatic

As Elisha disappeared from view, two she-bears came running out of the forest that approached the road on the opposite side. I jumped off the rock, hoping to escape up the hill away from the road. I expected the bears to leave us alone and soon return to the forest, but their every movement suggested aggression. No lumbering, lolloping movements either, such as I had seen with bears in the past; instead, they were among us within moments, making lightning-fast lunges at any boy within reach.

I was not the first to be struck, and from the screams that continued for what seemed like years afterwards, I must have been far from the last. But those two blows have taught me more than anything else in my life.

Was it just a random attack? Of course not. Nobody's fault? Nonsense.

I spent a lot of time with my face and hand bandaged. A lot of time unable to see, but still able to think. It was hard to admit, even to myself, that I had got what I deserved. I had known that what we were doing was wrong, and yet I had gone along with the crowd, joined in the worst of the jeering.

Now I had been cursed by Yahweh's prophet. Would the curse end with the disfigurement I had suffered, or was more punishment still to come?

None of the other boys seem to feel things the way I do. Given the chance, many of them would do just the same again – except that now they might take a sling with them for safety.

But I? I must seek forgiveness. I recognise my sin and desperately want to find the prophet and tell him that I

(https://openclipart.org/detail/462/attacking-bear)

have repented. Yahweh is the God of our fathers, and I want to worship him seriously from now on, not be cursed by him.

Will Elisha forgive me?

I have heard that he is at Samaria at the moment, and that is at least a day's walk away.

Even my parents don't really understand what I want to do, but they have given me permission anyway. Tomorrow, I am setting off for Samaria. I must find Elisha.

Six

To Serve a Prophet

For the true story, see 2 Kings 4:8-37; 5:1-27.

Sometimes it's a little creepy being the servant of one of God's prophets. Sometimes he knows what I am thinking, or can tell what I'm doing without needing to see it, but despite that, I wouldn't leave him for anything. I'm sure he needs my help, and I have to admit it – I need his help too.

Years ago, I had a chance to leave him and 'better myself'. Yes, I, Gehazi, the servant, could have set myself up as a wealthy, independent, landowner. I could have had servants of my own: menservants and maidservants, and later maybe, servants born in my house. It would have been Gehazi building a household of his own – but I'll get to that later.

You've probably never been a servant, so you wouldn't know what it's like. You've probably never seen my master, Elisha, either – though he is very famous, so maybe you have met him sometime: he's almost as famous as Elijah! In fact, he is known for doing almost twice as many miracles as that mighty hero ever did. But he doesn't look for fame – or money.

I started working for Elisha when I was very young. I must have been one of the luckiest teenagers in all of Israel, but my mother didn't think so at the time, and I suppose I didn't either for quite a while. You see, I came from a very poor family, and my mother never got over having to sell me as a servant. However, the sale earned my family enough money for them to be able to survive the drought, and it was a pretty bad drought – not as bad as the three-and-a-half year drought in Elijah's time,[6] nor the devastating seven year drought that came just a few years after I began to work for Elisha,[7] but bad enough that many died. My family didn't, thanks to the generous price Elisha paid for me.

So I swapped from working on our farm to working for Elisha. It took a while to get used to the idea of working indoors most of the time, though! It's not that we don't travel a lot too, but it was nothing like the work of ploughing and reaping and other jobs I was used to doing on the farm.

When I started working for Elisha, I had no idea what a prophet would be like. People are often rather superstitious about prophets, but I suppose I just expected that he would be much the same as any other man – only with a different sort of job from what I was used to.

However, it didn't take long for me to realise that he really was genuinely different from other people in a few ways. Now I suppose the fact that he was almost

---

[6] Luke 4:25; James 5:17-18 (see also 1 Kings 17:1; 18:1, 41-45)
[7] 2 Kings 8:1

completely bald was one difference from most other men, but that's not the sort of difference I mean. The important differences were all to do with his attitudes.

The biggest difference was that it was never possible to talk to him for very long without talking about Yahweh, our God. I guess it's a bit like me with Elisha: I am his servant, so he is never far from either my mind or my words. Well, Elisha is like that about God. If I meet people at the market, or on the road, and they want me to do something, I always have to take my master's wishes into account first – I can't just do what I want, or even what they want. And Elisha is genuinely like that with God.

Elisha works hard for God and he expects me to do the same. He also likes to help his fellow man and just occasionally he meets a person who can almost outdo him in that! There's a rich woman who lives in Shunem, and our involvement with her and her husband started because she was trying to help my master. At the time, we were passing through Shunem fairly often because Elisha travels around Israel in a circuit, visiting several towns and villages, just like Samuel the prophet used to do, so many years ago.[8] Now when I describe it as a circuit, it all sounds very simple – regular and organised – but a lot of the time, it wasn't quite so easy. Wherever we were, we would get messages from all sorts of places: those we were visiting next would ask if we could come sooner because there were problems that needed Elisha's wisdom to solve; the places we had just left would ask for us to come back so that Elisha could spell out one more detail of some judgement he had given; and still others would beg us to

---

[8] 1 Samuel 7:16

come to every possible place in Israel because Elisha was needed urgently.

One way or another, all of those requests meant that we were passing through Shunem quite often, and after a while this rich woman noticed and started to serve Elisha meals whenever he passed by. She even told him that if he was ever going past, at any time of day or night, we were to stop and enjoy her hospitality. Her husband is a generous man too, but it was clearly his wife who wanted to help in this way. It made the incessant travelling a little easier to bear, and may also have made Elisha a little more willing to travel in that area.

Then she upped the ante and suggested to her husband that they could build a small room on the roof for Elisha to stay in whenever we passed by.

The Shunammite woman and her husband built a room for Elisha to stay in whenever he passed by[9]

Now what is it that makes some people choose to be so generous? Certainly, she had the money to be able to

---

[9] http://freebibleimages.org/illustrations/elisha-boy/ Slide 3 (Sweet Publishing / FreeBibleImages.org, CC BY-SA 3.0 Unported)

afford her generosity, but there were many other rich people in the area, and none of them made the offer. Why was generosity so important to her, but not to others? There were only ever a few people in all the places where we travelled who welcomed us into their homes repeatedly, and of them all she was the most determined to welcome us – and all because Elisha was a man of God.

Our God has told us that he likes generosity, so it was very satisfying when he rewarded her with a wonderful blessing.

After quite a few visits where Elisha had stayed in the special room, he called her into the room during one visit and asked her how she would like to be repaid for her generosity. She replied, very simply and touchingly, that she was content with what she had. Who ever heard of anyone – let alone a rich person! – who was content with what they have? That was when I had a brainwave – I could tell just what she would like to have. So when she had left the room and we were discussing what we could do to help her, I pointed out to Elisha that she had no child. He connected the dots and immediately sent me to call her back into the room. As soon as he told her that she would have a child in about a year, it became very clear that this was the strongest desire she had in life; that her barrenness was her heaviest burden.

It was truly delightful to have been the instrument whereby God's special blessing could be given to a woman who had given so much to us. Her son was born the next year, just as Elisha had said, and the woman positively blossomed. She had always been a generous host, but after that, she was almost overwhelming in her gratitude.

I can't say it was a lesson I didn't already know, but it reinforced what I had seen before: God blesses people who are generous to others. They don't always become very rich or specially healthy or anything like that, but they are always blessed in one way or another.

So this woman seemed to float through life on a sea of happiness for a few years, but one day her happiness was torn apart, and her faith severely tested too. It was also a complete shock to my master and me.

We were staying on Mount Carmel at the time, and the first thing I knew about it was when Elisha suddenly said, "Look, there is the Shunammite." He thought for a few moments and then turned and said to me, "Run at once to meet her and say to her, 'Is all well with you? Is all well with your husband? Is all well with the child?' "

I had been washing my master's clothes, but I quickly dropped them and ran out to meet her. My master has amazing eyesight, and she was still right down in the Valley of Jezreel as I ran down the hill to meet her. She was riding on a donkey that was being led by a fit-looking young servant who was urging it to hurry. Clearly there was something important on her mind.

When I asked how things were going for her family and herself, she answered quietly, "All is well."

All I can say is that she didn't look as if all was well! However, it obviously wasn't me she wanted to talk to, so I led her up the mountain to where Elisha was waiting. Both the fit young man and the donkey were looking rather tired by the time we reached Elisha – it's not a short distance from Shunem to Mount Carmel.[10] All the way,

---

[10] From Shunem to Mount Carmel is about 35 km (22 miles).

she was obviously struggling inside, finding it hard not to collapse and weep, but absolutely determined to see Elisha.

When we arrived, she quickly climbed off the donkey, ran to my master, fell at his feet and grabbed at him.

Well, my master is a famous prophet, and we get some strange behaviour from women at times – young ones wanting to marry him and old ones wanting to mother him – but I didn't expect anything like that from the Shunammite! She had always been so sensible and serious. I suppose I was too hasty as I went to push her away, and Elisha quickly told me to be gentle with her. He said that she was obviously upset and that something terrible must have happened that God hadn't told him about. As usual, he was right. She deserved care from me, not criticism. I'm afraid that I'm a slow learner: quick to act and a bit slow to think. I try to learn, but it's hard. Without Elisha guiding me, I don't know where I would be.

With just a few words she showed what the problem was.

"Did I ask my lord for a son?" she asked. "Did I not say, 'Do not deceive me?'"

Without waiting to hear any more, Elisha recognised that something terrible had happened to her son, and ordered me urgently, "Tie up your garment and take my staff in your hand and go. If you meet anyone, do not greet him, and if anyone greets you, do not reply. And lay my staff on the face of the child."

I didn't even stop to pack anything or take any money – I just ran out of the door carrying Elisha's staff.

Everything was urgency that day, and I knew that I had a long journey in front of me: first down the mountain and then a gradual climb the rest of the way as I made my way up the valley of Jezreel towards Shunem.

I met several people on the way, and, oh! it was hard. But I pursed my lips and hurried on. Some of them even greeted me, but I just ran past them all in silence – except for my gasping breath. Never before had I just ignored people like that, and I hope I never have to again. Maybe that was why Elisha gave those instructions. I could have spent hours on the road exchanging news, as I normally do – particularly with the big bag of news I was carrying in my mind that day!

Hour after hour I hurried on, with no idea what I would find when I arrived. I outran both the donkey and that fit young man, but I was close to exhaustion when I finally stumbled up the road towards the Shunammite's house.

I climbed the stairs to the roof chamber and found the boy lying dead on Elisha's bed. By that time, he was quite cold to touch, but I obeyed my master and put the staff on his face.

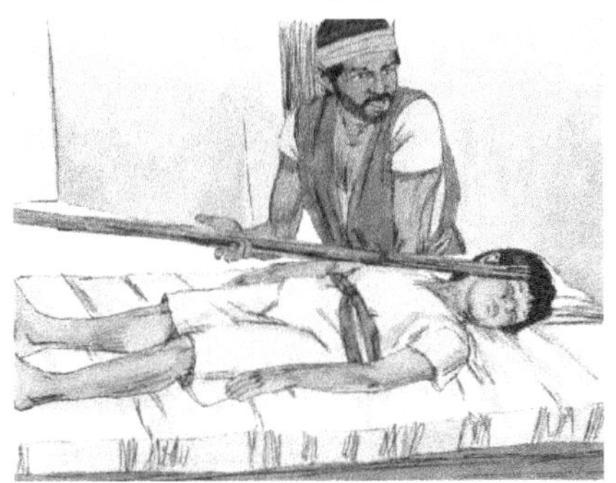

Gehazi went on ahead and laid the staff on the boy's face, but there was no response[11]

Naturally, I was hoping that the boy would take a sudden breath or even sit up and look at me, but nothing happened at all. I waited a little while just to see if something might be happening more slowly. Nothing did, but as I waited, the boy's father came into the room and asked what had happened. All he knew was that his wife had hurried off without explaining anything. He had finally asked the maidservants about his son just an hour before I arrived, and they had been able to report that their mistress and the servant had gone without the boy, so he must be somewhere about the house. A search had turned up nothing until they finally searched Elisha's room, and there they had found the lad, dead.

Trying to explain to the man what had happened wasn't easy, as I didn't know much myself. But at least I could tell the man where his wife was, and that Elisha the prophet was already on the way.

---

[11] http://freebibleimages.org/illustrations/elisha-boy/ Slide 12 (Sweet Publishing / FreeBibleImages.org, CC BY-SA 3.0 Unported)

I knew that the woman would be concerned about her son and that my master would want to know if his staff had made any difference – but would they want to know that it had done nothing? Or would that just make the woman's suffering worse? What should I do? It was a hard decision to make, especially while trying to ignore my extreme tiredness after running so far. Eventually, I decided to hurry back to meet my master. Every step was hard work, and the pain grew as I again ran most of the way. It took almost an hour to reach them, and by then I could hardly stand, let alone run! Gasping for breath, I told Elisha that the boy had not awakened despite my putting the staff on his face.

Seeing his worried response and the tears again springing to the eyes of the Shunammite, I felt that I had let them both down.

Then it was time to turn around yet again and hurry back to Shunem. As we walked, I could see that I wasn't the only exhausted one. The fit young man was looking all in and the poor donkey looked as if only stubbornness kept it going.

I was glad that it was summer time and the days long, but even so, darkness had well and truly fallen before our faltering steps brought us to the Shunammite's house. At the same time, the darkness made it a little easier to hide my utter exhaustion, though I believe that Yahweh gave me a little bit of extra strength for that last hour. Nevertheless, we were all very close to collapse as we climbed the stairs to Elisha's special room, wondering exactly what we would find. Elisha opened the door and we all craned our necks to see, but nothing had changed since I had hurried out of the room. The boy still lay there with the staff on his face.

Wasting no time, Elisha explained to us that he would go in alone and pray. The rest of us could, he said, wait outside.

So we did – at least, I was the only one who stayed waiting at the door. The Shunammite immediately went to find her husband and tell him what had happened, and the young servant staggered off to look after the tired donkey. Both man and beast had had a very hard afternoon's and evening's work. It occurred to me that both must appreciate their mistress greatly to be willing to work so hard to help her. I don't know if it is being a servant that makes me notice how other servants are treated, but notice I do!

Waiting was hard. From time to time, I would hear Elisha moving around, then silence would reign for a while. Suddenly I heard a sneeze, and I knew that it wasn't Elisha's sneeze! It must be the young boy – and then he sneezed again. And again. In fact, I think he sneezed seven times in all, and then I heard Elisha calling me. Eagerly I pulled the door open, and there was the lad, still lying on the bed, but now with his eyes open!

Elisha doesn't encourage me to ask him how he does such miracles – maybe he doesn't fully know himself – but this time he smiled at me almost with relief as I walked in with my mouth hanging open and a look of amazement on my face. I'm so lucky – blessed? – to have a master who shows me the power of God so often and reminds me that there is always more in this world than meets the eye. Later on he explained to me what had happened in the room, and it sounded as if that miracle was a great struggle for my master, although I'm not really sure how that works! At that moment, though, he wanted me to call the Shunammite, so I hurried down the stairs, stepping carefully in the darkness, and went to find her. I didn't want to steal my master's thunder by telling her that her son was alive again, but I did smile happily as I told her that my master wanted to see her − and I think she understood.

There was just one more thing about that wonderful day. It seemed little, but I don't think it was. Elisha presented the Shunammite with her son and said simply, "Pick up your son." But she didn't, or not straight away at least. First, she went and fell at Elisha's feet, bowing to the ground, and this time I wasn't so silly as to push her away. She simply had to express her thanks for the gift of her son, which had just been given to her for the second time. Thanking God was even more important to her than touching her newly-raised son.

A little thing? I don't think so.

Anyway, I'm no scribe, and I've spent so much time describing this incident that I don't have any left to write about any of the other amazing things that Elisha has done, except for the thing that led to the opportunity to better myself that I alluded to at the start.

☙

It seems strange to start by saying that one day, with no warning at all, I suddenly had a chance to become rich. I don't think that happens to many people.

However, I'm ashamed to admit that the only way I could get my hands on the money was to be a little deceitful. Of course, I wasn't cheating anyone out of anything they weren't willing to give, but there's no doubt it wasn't the best thing to do.

Naaman was the commander of the army of Syria and an exceptional leader, but he was also a leper. The king of Syria was willing to pay a huge amount of money to get Naaman cured by a prophet in Israel that he had heard about from a little slave girl. Of course, she must have been talking about my master, but neither the king of Syria nor Naaman knew who it was, so Naaman went to the king of Israel more or less demanding a cure – though he was willing to pay handsomely for it, in gold, silver and fine clothing.

It's quite a long story, but I'm really pressed for space, so I'll just say that Naaman eventually came to Elisha and was actually cured, after a bit of a false start. Then, as he was leaving, he tried to give all the money and clothes to my master – but he refused. All that money, just begging for a new owner, and Elisha was refusing it!

Now a workman who lives in his employer's house is typically paid about 10 shekels per year as well as his board. At that rate, Naaman was offering about 10,000 years' wages!

As soon as I heard the incredible offer and my master's even more incredible refusal, my mind began to search frantically for a way to get my hands on some of that money. Naaman urged Elisha again and again, but he was immovable. I was almost weeping in frustration by the time Naaman gave up and left.

Round and round in my head went the thought that Naaman had been let off lightly, and as I watched the party move off down the hill, I decided that I must not let them out of my sight. Somehow or other, I must go and get some of that money. I hate to admit it – because Elisha would say it was completely wrong – but I even took an oath in the name of Yahweh that I would get it.

I ran down the hill after them. I still didn't know what I could do, but I couldn't let all that beautiful money just walk away!

Then, just as I reached the bottom of the hill, a brainwave struck me, and I smiled as I ran after the Syrians. This would be easy.

And it was easy. Naaman saw me coming and stopped to wait. I explained that two of the sons of the prophets had just arrived and could my master have a talent of silver[12] and two changes of clothing? It wouldn't do to be greedy. Of course, it was all lies, but it worked. In fact, Naaman pressed me to take two talents[13] and I graciously conceded.

As I staggered back up the hill – carefully making sure that I stayed out of Elisha's sight – I dreamed of all that I could do with my newfound fortune in silver. Gehazi, the owner of olive orchards and vineyards, sheep and oxen, male servants and female servants, and dressed in fine clothes to suit my position of wealth.

I sneaked into the house and hid the money before going in to check on Elisha. It was hard to act as if things were normal, but I did my best.

It didn't help.

---

[12] One talent weighs 34.5 kilograms (76 pounds).
[13] Two talents weigh 69 kilograms (152 pounds).

As soon as I walked into the room, Elisha said, "Where have you been, Gehazi?"

"Your servant went nowhere," I said, cautiously.

But he said to me, "Did not my heart go when the man turned from his chariot to meet you? Was it a time to accept money and garments, olive orchards and vineyards, sheep and oxen, male servants and female servants? Therefore the leprosy of Naaman shall cling to you and to your descendants forever."

And that was it. Naaman's leprosy has been mine ever since. White as snow I walk through life, and strangers cringe from me. Those who know me understand that since I am white as snow with no raw flesh, my leprosy does not make me unclean, so I can move freely among the people,[14] but the stigma remains. Never can I forget my disease, or its cause.

Well, my time for writing is gone, and there is nothing more to say except to describe what happened to the money. Two talents of silver is a fortune, and it was all mine to dispose of. Elisha had made it clear that he didn't want it and that I shouldn't either. For some time I left the money untouched and it sat in its two bags in my room, reproaching me. Should I take it and lead a life of comfort on my own? Legally, I was committed to Elisha for the rest of my life, committed by the ceremony of awl and ear,[15] so to leave him would be to break my promise.

---

[14] Leviticus 13:12-15

[15] Deuteronomy 15:12-18 specified that a servant was to stay with his master for six years after which he was free to leave unless he chose to remain as a servant forever. Gehazi appears to have been Elisha's servant for more than six years so we assume that he chose to become a servant permanently.

This money had already led me into enough that was wrong, and I didn't want to add to the problem.

Finally I decided to give the money away. Elisha often had poor people coming to him begging for help, so it wasn't hard to find a demand for the money. Gradually, I managed to get rid of it all.

It was hard to give away all that money, piece by piece, watching my hope of security and comfort slipping through my fingers, but I'm sure it was worth it. I have to admit it: I haven't needed it.

Seven

Hosea's Story

For the true story, see Hosea 1-2. Much of the story is guesswork. The guesses have been based on the idea that the relationship between Hosea and Gomer is a picture of the relationship between God and Israel.

I loved her. I still love her. Yet I only married her because God told me to. And after she left me, I only bought her back again because God told me to.

Our marriage has been a mixture of highs and lows. The highs have been wonderful, but short-lived. The lows have been devastating times of betrayal and abandonment.

Words cannot describe how at times she has torn my heart to shreds and then brutally encouraged others to dance on the pieces. Over time, each time, I have recovered – but then it happens all over again.

☙

My life seemed quite pleasant and well organised until one night the word of God came to me, and from then on everything was turned upside down. True, I didn't have a wife, but Solomon makes it plain in his proverbs that if you can't find the right wife, you are better off without one.

But God's command that night was the most shocking instruction that I have ever heard of, and...

Well, I really need to set the scene more clearly so that you can understand how it all happened – and just how close to impossible obedience was.

Before that night, I had never heard from God directly. I believed in God and did my best to obey his commands and the laws he had given, but I had never personally heard his voice.

Hearing the voice of God for the first time would have been shock enough, but it was what God said that made the event so deeply distressing and left me in an agony of doubt.

"Marry a prostitute and have children of prostitution," said God, "because the land commits great prostitution by forsaking Yahweh."

As an unmarried but chaste and faithful servant of God, this instruction was simply impossible to accept. God's law told us about purity and holiness, and I had coveted these characteristics all my life. Were not prostitutes to be executed under God's law? If a new wife was found not to be a virgin, had not God himself commanded that she be stoned?[16]

It was impossible. Something must be wrong. The voice I had heard in my head must be creeping insanity. Maybe I had misunderstood somehow, or maybe I had

---

[16] Deuteronomy 22:13-21

missed a few words: "Whatever you do, don't…" But nothing that I thought of could explain the dilemma in which I now found myself.

I wouldn't do it. I couldn't do it. God would never expect me to do it – in fact, it would be sin if I obeyed!

I don't know if you can put yourself in my position at all – I suppose you really can't – but just imagine how you would feel if God told you to go and do something you knew was completely against his rules. That's how I felt.

"Marry a prostitute" – I just couldn't. No matter how often I write it, it doesn't begin to compare with the number of times the sentences went through my head: "I won't! I can't – it's wrong!"

I decided to sleep on it, but then I spent the rest of that night praying for understanding. The next day, I fasted. I meditated and tried to find excuses.

After a few days, I spoke to my father and mother about it, and they were horrified. They agreed with me and with each other that it was completely out of the question. God would not, could not, want me to do such a thing. I must have got something about God's message wrong. I was getting all the support I could want – except for God's. He had spoken, and I knew it. I couldn't really have any doubts that the command was from God, however repulsive, revolting, disgusting, offensive, vile, abominable, appalling, foul and nauseatingly stomach-turning it was.

Then I thought that maybe if I waited, God would see how objectionable it was to me and let me off. So I waited, but nothing happened....

And so it went on. I delayed, I argued, I got support from my friends and family. I did everything I could think of to avoid the entire unspeakable business. But the words of God just sat in my mind and smouldered.

☙

In the end, I gave in and decided to do what I was told, but it was indescribably hard.

But where was I to start with such a task? I began by deciding that if God wanted me to do this, he would make it work. Somehow. It was an important decision, and without it, I don't think I could have kept going.

Then I thought to myself, "I don't know any prostitutes, so how do I find one to marry?" Suddenly, it occurred to me that there was that girl, Gomer, the daughter of Diblaim, who used to live down the street. I had never quite known what had happened to her, but there had been a time when no-one respectable had ever spoken to her, and then she had gone and I had not seen her since.

It didn't take many enquiries to find out that she could be the very person I was looking for. I still cringed at the idea, but since I had decided to go ahead, I followed up the information I had found. Gomer now lived in a house near one of the gates in the north of the city – close enough to the gate for visiting men to find her, but far enough from the temple to avoid temple officers or others who might want to enforce the law if they saw her.

Over the last few years, I have learned a lot about the immorality that can go on right under the noses of righteous people, even when mostly faithful kings like

Uzziah are in power. It has shown me that God was quite right in his comment about the land forsaking him.

How does one get to know a whore? I wasn't willing to pay her or to become promiscuous myself. So how could I get to know her? I couldn't really just knock on her door and ask her to marry me.

Further inquiries revealed that she lived in a house with two other women who were also prostitutes. Next door there was an inn which also provided food and lodgings for visitors to the city. Apparently this inn had a cosy arrangement with the prostitutes which allowed them to pick up customers from the eating areas as long as the inn received a commission.

That night, I went to the inn for a meal to see if I could meet Gomer. Thoughts of her had filled my mind and I had been searching my memory for any picture of her, though without success.

As I sat by the wall eating my meal and watching, a woman entered. At once I recognised Gomer. She was a small, innocent-looking young woman with raven-black hair and an attractive figure. Her face was pleasant without being beautiful, and as she looked around the room, our eyes met. A sort of puzzled recognition lit up her eyes, as if she recognised me but was not sure how. I did my best to smile, but I don't think I was very successful. I felt overwhelmed by the idea that I was looking at a woman of a sort whom, in the past, I would never have talked to or even met, but whom I was now thinking of marrying!

Gomer smiled at me and I was surprised how much it hurt. Why should I care that she had smiled at many other men in the same way, and why should it matter that the smile showed no genuine pleasure in meeting me? I pushed the feeling away and tried to smile again while patting the seat beside me. She took the hint, walking across to where I sat and sitting down beside me.

"Gomer, do you remember me?" I asked, feeling foolish.

"I feel as if I do, but when would I have met you before? Have you... have we..." she left the question hanging and I quickly interjected.

"You lived near us a few years ago – before you moved here," I said.

"Oh, yes," she said cautiously, looking a little embarrassed. It seemed that she felt awkward mixing a past life of innocence with her current business.

"Are you happy in your work, Gomer?" I asked, finding, unexpectedly, that I cared about her answer.

"Do you know the work I do?" she asked, looking at me challengingly. I nodded slowly and she continued, looking down at her hands in her lap, "It is work. I earn more money than I would doing anything else." She looked up at me and added, "But some of the customers can be difficult."

"Is there anyone who can help you with any problems?" I asked. She looked so small and defenceless as she sat next to me.

"No, it's all up to me," she replied, shrugging her shoulders. A strong desire to care for her and protect her came over me, and it was with difficulty that I prevented myself from saying anything about it.

We talked for a while about her work – in very general terms – until a man dressed in fine clothes entered the room. Gomer noticed him first, and clearly recognised him. He sat down and glanced dismissively at me before looking familiarly at Gomer. Jealousy filled me and I compressed my lips, shaking my head in anger. Trying to control myself, I asked quickly, "Will you eat with me, Gomer?"

She looked a little confused, but agreed, casting an apologetic smile at the richly dressed customer.

It felt like a victory, and I arranged a meal for her as quickly as I could. While it was being prepared, we talked about the area where we had both lived, and I did all I could to find out about her earlier life. She answered my questions simply and clearly, although some of her answers were horrific. As the youngest of six children, her parents had been pre-occupied with her older brothers and sisters and had had no real interest to spare for her. Used more as a domestic slave than a daughter, she had worked hard for very little food and no love. She even admitted that the suggestion that she become a prostitute had come from her father.

We talked for a long time, and as we talked I felt my desire to do whatever I could to help and look after her strengthening. She needed protection, and I wanted to provide it. I was falling in love.

At some time during the evening, the rich customer gave up and left, but neither of us noticed it. It was very late when I left. As I stood up to leave and said my goodbyes, Gomer seemed first surprised and then disappointed. At the time, I was pleased, thinking only that she was disappointed that I was leaving. It was not until later that it occurred to me that her disappointment might have been due to a lack of income for the evening.

I returned on other evenings, but Gomer never again spent such a long time with me. She seemed to enjoy my company and to look forward to my visits, but at some stage during each evening, she would start looking around at the others in the room and make some excuse or other to leave. Every time I watched her slim form leaving me, I wished that I could care for her so that she would have no need to seek income from sin. Invariably, jealousy filled me and I left as quickly as possible, knowing what she was seeking, but not wanting to know any more about it.

One evening, she was quieter than usual and seemed distracted as we sat down together.

"What is wrong, Gomer?" I asked, concerned.

"It doesn't matter, I can cope," she replied, trying to smile.

"Is there anything I can do to help?" I asked. "I would like to have the opportunity to help you."

"Why?" she asked, looking utterly lost. Maybe she had never before had anyone who loved her.

"Because I love you and would like to look after you, Gomer," I replied.

"Why?" she asked again, looking even more lost and confused.

"I want you to be my wife, Gomer. Will you marry me?"

She began to protest, "But I am a…" but I stopped her, holding up both hands. I didn't want to be reminded of that.

"Will you marry me?" I asked again, pleadingly. "I can look after you and you won't need to do that any more. We can be happy together and faithful to each other."

"I like you, Hosea," she said. "I have always enjoyed our conversations. And I can be a good wife to you."

Hosea married Gomer[17]

"Will you marry me?" I asked for a third time, eagerly this time.

"Yes," she said, smiling into my eyes and putting her hand on mine. Then she looked around at the customers and I could sense what was coming.

"No, Gomer," I said firmly. "When I leave tonight, you are coming with me. There is to be no more of this… this… working," I finished, lamely.

---

[17] http://freebibleimages.org/illustrations/hosea/ Slide 2 (Arabs for Christ / FreeBibleimages.org, CC BY-SA 3.0 Unported)

That night, I took her with me when I left and led her straight to my parents' house. They greeted her coldly and it was clear that they knew exactly who she was and what she was. I couldn't believe how much my own attitude had changed, since I would previously have felt precisely the same as they did. Now I felt protective, and spoke firmly to my parents about how they must treat my betrothed wife. Very kindly and generously they did so, and we were married shortly afterwards.

ℭℜ

The start of our married life was happy. I loved Gomer and she loved me. We had each promised to be faithful to each other, and she had promised particularly that she would never work as a prostitute again.

Had it not been for God's comments about unfaithfulness, I would have been sure that our marriage would be happy and fulfilling for the rest of our lives. If I had been truly convinced of this, later events would have been even harder to accept than they were. But in the back of my mind, Israel's words at Mount Sinai echoed mockingly:

"All the words that the Lord has spoken we will do."[18]

Soon after our wedding, Gomer was expecting our first child. I was filled with joy and Gomer was quite pleased too, although for some time her pleasure was curbed by morning sickness.

How happy we were together when our son was born. Then God told me to name him Jezreel because God was

---

[18] Exodus 24:3

soon going to punish the ruling house of Jehu because of the blood shed when Jehu had demanded the deaths of the many sons of Ahab in the town of Jezreel.[19]

Gomer did not like the name: she said it was negative and unpleasant.[20] Why couldn't we just give him a "normal" name like other people did? She felt that it was all very well to worship Yahweh as a god, but that having him name our children seemed peculiar. Nothing I could say would change her opinion, and a gulf began to open between us. This was not the first sign of difficulties ahead, but it was the most significant.

When I look back, I can see that she was already pining for her old days of freedom – as she saw it. Freedom to live without constraint, without limits.

Jezreel grew quickly and was healthy and happy. I spent as much time with him as I could, given my uncertainty about his mother. I still loved her and did whatever I could to help her and show her my love, but within just a few months, she began going out by herself regularly, leaving young Jezreel with me to look after.

I tried to stop her going. I reminded her of her past and her promises, but she assured me that she was doing nothing wrong. She declared that she loved me and would always be faithful to me. I wanted to believe her, and we still had pleasant times together when she was at home. Could I trust her? Our neighbours started to notice her behaviour, and some were kind enough to come and warn me about what was happening.

---

[19] 2 Kings 10:1-9

[20] Jezreel means "God will disperse".

I was desperate. I tried speaking to a friend and asking for his wife to talk to Gomer about what was happening. In their loving helpfulness, they did so, but Gomer had innocent explanations for everything she did. So I followed Gomer myself one day, and what I saw made me wish that I hadn't. It did take away my doubts, but that didn't really help. Gomer was my wife: what should I do? She was abandoning me and our son, but I could not abandon her.

The owner of the inn where I had met Gomer was not a godly man, but I had got to know him quite well while I had been going there to see Gomer. I decided to speak to him to see whether there was any way in which he could discourage her from going to his inn. I had already been hurt and angry, but after speaking with him I felt savage. He reported that Gomer had told him that I was quite happy with her behaviour and that she had my permission to return to her old habits of prostitution.

At that moment, if I had met any of the men she went to the inn to see, I would assuredly have killed them. If I had met Gomer, I honestly don't know what I would have done, but I'm glad that I didn't. It was only once I went home and thought bitterly about God's requirements for me that my jealousy and anger began to lose their grip.

I started to see that what Gomer was doing to me was just what my nation had always done to God. We had promised eternal obedience and faithfulness, only to quickly break our word by disobeying God's commands and worshipping other gods. Not only that, but we had claimed that we were still worshipping faithfully, and that we had God's approval for our behaviour.

It wouldn't be true to say that I began to feel a long patience with my beloved but unfaithful wife: my jealousy continued to burn furiously within me, and I couldn't control the terrible pain that seemed to tear at me endlessly. But it wasn't as bad as it had been, and the realisation made me determined to keep trying as God does.

That night, Gomer came home early, feeling unwell. As I looked at her closely, I guessed why, but said nothing. The next morning, she was nauseous and ill, and this continued for about two months.

During all that time, I helped her when she could not even stand without vomiting, and looked after Jezreel all of the time when ordinarily I would have been winning bread for the family. God showed us his love and kindness by providing food for the family, and I struggled to emulate his patience. Gomer was pathetically grateful for my care and persistently repentant. Once again, the similarity with my nation was clear: throughout our history, we had wilfully abandoned God again and again, only to crawl back to him when we needed his help.

We both knew that it was morning sickness that was making her feel uncomfortable, and both of us had questions about that.

Once the morning sickness had passed, Gomer stayed grateful and content for a few months, but before the child was born, she was clearly chafing again, and it was only her physical awkwardness that kept her at my side.

Our second child, a girl, was finally born – but was she ours?[21] God told me to name her "Lo-ruhamah",

---

[21] Hosea 2:4 says that Gomer's children were children of prostitution,

which means "no mercy", and Gomer wasn't happy with that either. She was very pleased to have a daughter, but the name she would not accept. Instead, Gomer called her "Racham", which meant the exact opposite of God's name for her. Where would this lead, I wondered? I made sure that I used God's name for our daughter, but her mother always responded that she embodied love and compassion and was lacking nothing. God's unending fight with my nation was being acted out in my family as good was said to be evil and evil, good.

Could the situation get any worse, I asked myself? But it seemed that it could. Soon after Lo-ruhamah's birth, Gomer was straying again, but now she took Lo-ruhamah with her every time. Short of beating her or locking her up, there was nothing I could do. At times, I made sure that I took Jezreel and Lo-ruhamah out with me before Gomer left, but whenever I did so, she was aggressive and abusive when we next met. She began to mock me and tell me horrible things about her behaviour, doing her best to hurt me and make me let her have her own way. When I had recovered from her cruelty and could think clearly, I could see the similarities between her behaviour and Israel's flagrant presentation of idolatry before the children whom God had given, and even in our worship of God.

What should I do? God had not abandoned his people over centuries – should I be abandoning my wife after only four years of marriage? Oh, but it hurt so much: could I keep going?

---

but there is no specific comment about Lo-ruhamah's paternity.

∞

After a while, Gomer weaned Lo-ruhamah and began to demand that she be able to leave the child at home while she wandered abroad looking fruitlessly for love and happiness.

Naturally, this made life very difficult for me, since I had to care for the two children while still providing food for us all – including their mother. The money Gomer earned from her activities never made it into the family coffers. It was always spent on her or her customers: clothes, jewellery, wine, cosmetics, and anything else that suited her.

After a short while, however, Gomer was pregnant again, and that time I had no doubt: her child was not mine.[22] Gomer made no effort to hide the fact, discussing it openly with me, our neighbours and even Jezreel, who was four years old by that time. Can words ever fully describe this sort of betrayal and callous abuse?

Gomer was still living in my home when her second son was born, and God told me to name him "Lo-ammi", which means "Not My People". Gomer was deeply offended by this name, telling me indignantly that it announced to everyone that she was an unfaithful wife! Yes, she really was upset, and she really did say that. I had seen a lot of hypocrisy from Gomer before, but this was beyond belief. I was so utterly shocked and speechless that my mouth dropped open as she told me, and this further infuriated her. As usual, her anger was expressed

---

[22] Hosea 2:4 says that Gomer's children were children of prostitution, but there is no specific comment about Lo-ammi's paternity.

in sneering, contemptuous disdain and savagely disparaging comparisons of me with her favourites.

Nothing got better after that, and the first year or two of Lo-ammi's life were very similar to the same period in Lo-ruhamah's life. My dilemma was just as painful. After knowing Gomer for seven years, I was still in love with her, despite the constant advice of my parents, relatives and friends to divorce her and separate my family from her contemptible behaviour. Should I follow their advice? Should I send her away?

℘

Then Gomer took the matter out of my hands. She left me.

It was not that I was being cruel or unreasonable. I asked nothing of her that she had not already promised to give, and for my part, I tried to give her everything that I had promised: faithfulness, love and oneness. All that I had was hers. Whatever I could give, I gave. Her children I treated as my children, even the two I was sure were the results of her prostitution.

Nevertheless, she left me. She took all that I had given her: the goods, the money, and her three children – yes, even Jezreel, my son – and moved out of our home. I was left completely alone.

It sounds utterly stupid, but even then, I still loved her. I knew where to find her and visited frequently to beg her to return. At times she would almost agree, only to break her word at the last minute. I threatened and cajoled by turns, but nothing worked. She didn't know it, but I even continued to pay her living expenses so that she could have food to eat instead of only the soul-destroying wines and perfumes she befuddled her brain with.

Nothing worked.

But the break was not complete, because she still announced herself to others as "the wife of Hosea", and even called me her "lord". She made me look foolish as a man who was promised faithfulness but was willing to accept flagrant betrayal instead.

Whenever I stopped to think, I couldn't believe what I was doing. But when I thought a bit more, I saw how God had treated my people, my ancestors, and how he treats me.

In those times of despair, God spoke to me with messages for his people, and I felt a strong empathy with the helpless litany of God's suffering due to our unfaithfulness, deception and treachery as a nation.

The nights were the worst, because I knew what she would be doing and worried about what would be happening to her children. Whenever there was a feast day for one of the terrible idols that so many in Israel worshipped, I knew that Gomer would be there, mixing with the worshippers and seeking money in any way that she could get it. And I was always terrified that one day I would find that her children had joined the queue of panic-stricken and helpless boys and girls who were taken by their parents to be sacrificed in the bloodthirsty cults of Baal and Molech. Thankfully she never did that, limiting herself to sacrificing her own humanity in those debauched celebrations.

This heartbreak went on for years. From time to time I met Gomer or her children in the market. The children were growing up and Gomer herself was looking much older. A life of prostitution is never a happy life, but she could not see what it was doing to her. She would not listen.

Then one day I met Jezreel in the market. By that time he was about twelve or thirteen years old and looked more like a young man than a boy.

"Jezreel!" I said eagerly, and he looked at me doubtfully. He knew that I was his father, but Gomer had always told him that I was unfair and demanding, so it was hard for him to welcome conversation with me. Undaunted, I continued, "Peace to you, Jezreel. May God bless you."

"Hello, father," he replied carefully. "What do you want?"

"I want to get to know you again, Jezreel," I answered. "You are my son and I love you."

He shook his head to dismiss my mention of love and said, "I don't think that I will be able to see you very often. Mother is arranging for me to enter service in the worship of Baal, and that will keep me very busy."

It was an unbearable shock to hear my son speaking so casually about such a loathsome future, and I wondered whether he really knew what was planned for him. I had no doubt that he would be made into one of the cult prostitutes that God had condemned at every opportunity. My own son! How could this be happening?

He saw my shocked reaction and asked, "What's wrong, father? I know that you don't like Baal, but surely being dedicated to worship is not a bad thing?"

"The worship of Baal is always a bad thing, and becoming a cult prostitute is almost infinitely worse! It is utterly evil, there is nothing good in it at all. Please come and live with me and learn to love Yahweh our God."

"Mother didn't mention anything about becoming a cult prostitute," he answered. "I don't like the sound of that. I'll have to ask her."

"I will come with you," I said.

"Oh, no," he answered, waving his hand in refusal. "Mother has always said that we must not bring you home if we ever meet you. She says that she will not see you unless you wish to see her as part of her work."

I cannot describe the pain that I felt hearing these words from the mouth of my son. It was a calculated and brutal insult from the woman I still loved, innocently delivered by the son I also loved. I shook my head to try to get rid of the pain, but it didn't help.

"Very well," I agreed finally, "I will not see her now. But please give her a message from me. I am begging her to stop her prostitution. Stop her unfaithfulness. While she behaves like this, she is not my wife, and I am not her husband. I want her to come back to me."

"I will tell her," said Jezreel in a wooden voice that was devoid of any emotion.

"And you, Jezreel, please, come and live with me. You are my son and you will receive mercy from me."

We parted and I went home to weep and pray. My son! Could I save him from the terrible fate his mother was condemning him to?

CR

Jezreel did speak to his mother and she admitted that the "service to Baal" that she had planned for him was indeed for him to become a cult prostitute. Although he did not consider the job to be wrong as such – he had no real ideas of right and wrong – he really wanted to become a shepherd or a herdsman, something working with animals.

Despite bitter resistance from Gomer, Jezreel eventually came to live with me. A few months later, I was able to find a shepherd living near Jerusalem who was willing to take Jezreel on and teach him his skills. When he was not needed in the fields, Jezreel stayed with me, and I gradually taught him more about Yahweh and convinced him that he really was one of God's children.

One small victory had been won after fourteen years of struggle, and I still didn't know where it might lead.

Gomer had rejected my request that she return to me, and had kept the other two children with her. Probably she found them useful for the housework. However, after her treatment of Jezreel, I was terrified that she would use them for much worse things than housework. Still, there was nothing I could do.

The years passed slowly, and I gradually began to win other small victories. Gomer's situation got steadily worse. She was ageing quickly, and in her job that was disastrous. Over the next few years, first Lo-ruhamah and then Lo-ammi came to live with me, and I did my best to care for them and introduce them to the wonders of worshipping a living God. Over the years, I also made countless offers to Gomer, but she would never return to me – being willing even to lose access to her children rather than do so.

Finally, Gomer slipped even lower, if that was possible, and lived with a man who said that he loved her, but hired her out as a prostitute whenever he wanted more money.

I was almost heartbroken when I heard the details. Then, as I prayed to God about it, he spoke to me with an instruction that was just what I wanted in some ways, but very worrying in others. God told me to buy Gomer from the man who "loved" her. I did so, paying a high price for her in silver and barley, but specified to her the conditions of the purchase: "You must dwell as mine for a long time. You shall not be a prostitute, or belong to another man, and I will also belong to you."

Gomer's position by then was so dire that she agreed to my conditions, and we all lived together once again as a family – except for Jezreel, who now worked in the fields as a shepherd.

Over time, Gomer's bitterness against me slowly wore off. She came to see the benefits of faithfulness, and finally there was a day when, suddenly, she recognised her own faults and no longer blamed them on either God or me. For the first time ever, she admitted her guilt to herself, and to me, and I was very thankful that I was there to console and encourage her. It took some time for her to really accept that both God and I could forgive her, but from that time on she was a completely changed person.

All of the characteristics that I had seen as tiny beautiful shoots within her when she was young – and loved on sight – now grew and matured into a varied character of great loveliness.

Gomer became a tireless worker for good, helping, advising, teaching and guiding people towards godliness. Her children forgave her, and were glad to follow her new example. She began to look younger and younger, and her entrancing smile gradually re-emerged as she recovered from many years of abusing the body God had given her. Healing came with her new faith. Together, we have found a happiness that grows greater with each passing year.

For me, the journey through despair and the valley of darkness took more than twenty years. For God, the suffering continues, as his nation still despises him and treats him with the contempt Gomer showed me for so many years. Our marriage has been a parable, and our happiness now is a prophecy of the time when God will welcome Israel back as a nation that loves him from a pure and obedient heart.

It will come, just as it has come for us.

Eight

The Blind Leading the Blind

For the true story, see 2 Kings 17:24-41.

It's good to be back home. Back in a land of hills and valleys; of forests and vineyards; of rain and sunshine. When the Assyrians finally captured Samaria, they carried us all into exile, scattering us right across their empire. That was their policy: split up each nation into small groups and spread them everywhere, then they won't ever get organised enough to rebel.

I was taken to a small town near the Habor River. The number of exiles sent to each place was carefully chosen so that we knew just enough people in the town to feel almost at home, but at the same time were surrounded by enough other people that we would feel outnumbered, intimidated and uncomfortable.

I spent a year there and I was glad to leave.

And now, back here in Israel, I have an important job to do.

When the Assyrians took us away, they brought in people from Babylon, Cuthah, Avva, Hamath, and Sepharvaim and settled them throughout our cities. As you can imagine, when they arrived, they lived in the same way as they were used to living in their own countries – and that completely ignored Yahweh, the God of Israel, which is a *really* bad idea.

New idols were springing up everywhere. The men of Babylon made Succoth-benoth, the men of Cuth made Nergal, the men of Hamath made Ashima, and the Avvites made Nibhaz and Tartak; and the Sepharvites burned their children in the fire to Adrammelech and Anammelech, the gods of Sepharvaim.

You get the picture. It was a free-for-all. But it didn't include Yahweh.

Well, everything seemed to be going fine, until lions started killing some of the people. Of course, I can't say for sure that it was Yahweh who did it – it may have been just that having fewer people in the land had allowed the number of lions to increase – but *they* were certain it must be because they weren't worshipping the local god properly. So they made enquiries and found out that his name was Yahweh.

That was when an urgent call came to bring back one of the priests who had been carried away, and I was the lucky one chosen.

It is delightful to be back in Israel, even if most of the people here now speak languages I can't understand. At least I am back in Israel, the land where I was born.

Communicating has been a bit of a problem too. I suppose one of the reasons I was chosen is that I speak a few languages quite well, including Aramaic, and fortunately quite a few of the new inhabitants speak Aramaic, so I can converse reasonably with them, at least.

The afternoon I arrived in Bethel, the news had just arrived that a man had been killed by a lion that very morning. It made me popular, I can tell you: everyone was hanging on my every word, expecting me to tell them how to solve the problem – and hurry up about it!

There was a feast that night, and straight away they asked me if Yahweh had any requirements for the food they should eat. I was able to reassure them that although some people put restrictions on what people could eat and claimed that the rules came from Yahweh, we had not paid much attention to any rules like that in modern times, and, well, I was still alive!

All this expectation put a lot of pressure on me, too. Of course I can teach them how to worship Yahweh alright – no-one better – but will that solve the problem?

When I was a long way away and happy to grasp at any opportunity to get back home, even if only for a while, it was all very well to agree that their failure to worship Yahweh must be the problem – but it was quite another matter standing in front of an audience who expected me to solve the lion problem in double-quick time. And I wasn't sure that I could! All I could do was to teach them about Yahweh and hope that the problem would go away – whatever the reason for it might be.

Thankfully, I had done some preparation on the way, writing myself some lists of things that I needed to teach them about worshipping Yahweh.

This was the list I started with. Seven points, with a short explanation for each:

• **Yahweh is the God of Israel:** the nation, yes, but also the location. People who live in Israel must acknowledge Yahweh. Hence the lions.

• **Visible representations of God are necessary**, otherwise people concentrate on the worship of other gods that have gaudy displays. Hence the golden calves.

• **Elevated places are best for the grander aspects of religion.** Religion is vital and should have a prominent position of authority. Elevated positions are closer to heaven where Yahweh lives and they promote a "big picture" view of life and religion. Hence the high places scattered all over Israel.

• **Quiet, private clearings under green trees are the best places for worship in relation to the more earthy aspects of religion** – matters in which we acknowledge our links to the living, reproducing world around us. This is one of the areas where the worship of Yahweh can integrate well with the worship of other deities that more fully unlock these areas of human experience. Hence the sites for shared worship in many places throughout Israel, with their private booths and sacred assistants.

• **Feasts are celebrations of God's blessings and times for us to really let our hair down.** I won't spell out what goes on. You can use your imagination. We Israelites always knew that God wanted us to be happy. Down in the south, they seem to celebrate gloominess, but we don't have that problem. Hence, people always came to *our* feasts.

- **Be careful of so-called scriptures, prophets and those who exclude others from worship.** In particular, avoid those who claim that Yahweh insists on obedience, humility and suchlike. The nation of Judah is full of such people. They will tell you they are holier than you are. Hence the rules about not going to Jerusalem for worship.

- **Worship is for everyone,** and people are all different. Yahweh knows our differences and allows us to worship other gods as well as himself, as long as we acknowledge him. Hence the proliferation of idols, altars, temples and shrines throughout the land.

They worshipped however they wanted[23]

Obviously the worship of Yahweh has developed over time. Cultural changes have come to Israel over the centuries and our religion has moved with the times – just as it did way back when we left Egypt. After all, if we don't pay attention to keeping our religion up to date, we really aren't doing our duty to God. Old-fashioned worship

---

won't be attractive to the younger generation, and staid, serious worship won't attract the more lively people either. With just a little bit of imagination and creativity, the worship of God can be made attractive to everyone.

So I taught them how we worshipped, and naturally, they wanted to know what careers were available in this religion – in fact, there were already a few candidates who were interested in a religion whose God could send lions to punish. I was pleased to be able to assure them that anyone can be a priest of Yahweh as long as they have the appropriate training, and to some extent, that's what I was there for, too.

I won't be surprised if there are even more applicants if the lions *do* stop killing people once they begin to worship Yahweh. We shall have to wait and see.

CR

Today I'm packing up to leave. I have been here for almost a year now, teaching and explaining, selecting and ordaining new priests of Yahweh. All of them have a healthy fear of Yahweh because of those lions, but they have also maintained a healthy variety of worship in their private lives and a pleasing tolerance for the cultural differences of others – there is no mindless insistence on exclusive or rule-based worship.

The lions have stopped killing their people, too, so maybe it really was Yahweh sending the lions. Maybe.

When I get back to that town on the Habor River – I still can't really call it "home" – I'll have to think about that a bit more. If Yahweh really can send lions, should that change our attitude to him? We've always treated

Yahweh with respect, but, honestly, we haven't highlighted it. We've tended to treat him more like an optional extra god, even a gentle grandfather god, but maybe he's a bit more than that. As I say, I'll try to spend some time thinking about it once I get back. It's not urgent.

Yesterday all the new priests were gathered together to say goodbye. They asked me for some parting words of wisdom: a pithy summary of what they should do to make sure that the lions stay away.

Yet again, preparation had made my job easier, because I had already planned a closing statement. I wrote it down for them:

"Worship Yahweh as the Israelites did – obviously it worked since we weren't being killed by lions."

Nine

Repentance and Forgiveness

For the true story, see 2 Kings 21:1-18 and 2 Chronicles 33:1-20.

How could I have been such a fool? And for so long? My father, Hezekiah, was loving and good. Everyone thought he was wonderful and admired his faith.

Yet the moment I became king I worked as hard as I could to undo every good thing he ever did.

I'm going to go through a list of some of the things I did, without trying to excuse myself. Here is a list of some of my evil practices:

- I worshipped dead idols all over Jerusalem and filled the city with altars dedicated to them.

- I put altars to those idols in both courts of the temple of Yahweh.

- I put an Asherah pole in Yahweh's temple.

- I called fortune tellers every day to try to glean hints of the future from them.

- I used mediums and necromancers so that I could talk to the dead and get information that no-one else had.

- I frequently used magicians and wizards to put curses on people and perform other magic.
- I ignored everything said by God's prophets, and killed many of them.
- I ignored everything said by the priests of Yahweh.
- I killed many of Yahweh's priests who spoke against me.
- I killed many people in Jerusalem who opposed me.
- I killed many people in Jerusalem who tried to serve God even if they did nothing against me.
- I even killed my own sons (yes, several of them) in the fires of the Valley of the Son of Hinnom as offerings to various idols.

Overall, I reigned with a reign of terror. I filled Jerusalem from end to end with blood. The blood of righteous people and knaves, of God's servants and his enemies. I have no idea how many people were killed at my command or as a result of my attitudes and the brutal friends I cultivated.

This, however, is only a list of some of the wrong things I did. It makes no mention of the things I should have done but did not do. My father did not just avoid evil things: he did good things.

So on both sides of the coin, I went wrong.

I cannot explain what it is like to feel that everybody in my kingdom has known the death of relatives or friends, just because of me. Everybody, from the servants who clean my floors to the gatekeepers who greet me as I pass. Everyone I meet on the street and everyone who cooks my food. No-one has escaped my vicious brutality.

I cannot explain how it feels to have led everybody in my kingdom away from Yahweh to the bloodthirsty worship of empty idols. Nobody who worshipped Yahweh has been allowed to do so without my best efforts being expended towards leading them into different worship.

No man who maintained a clean life and clean speech was left alone. My men would bring such innocents before me and we would do our best to degrade their morals and their language. If they refused to laugh at our vile jokes, they would be immediately punished and we would try again. Not very many refused to obey my commands, so most pure men were led to impurity by me. Any who did utterly reject my demands, died: possibly they were the only ones who benefited from my rulership. At least they maintained their faith.

Faithful husbands were encouraged and threatened into unfaithfulness. Women were molested and perversion promoted. And all at my insistence.

This continued for more than 40 years.

And then, suddenly, it happened. Without warning, a rather small army from Assyria marched straight through Israel and arrived at the undefended walls of Jerusalem. I was busy offering sacrifices to Baal and Ashtoreth as the commanders of Assyria marched in through the open gates of Jerusalem.

I was seized in the temple of Yahweh which I had stolen and used for my own gods – not one of which could protect me when I needed it. I was publicly humiliated in the courts.

The Assyrians put a hook through Manasseh's nose[24]

I felt a little of the suffering I had inflicted on so many as a large sharpened hook was pushed through my nose. It was agony and I had no idea what would happen next – was I to be killed in the sort of torture for which the Assyrians are justly famous? A chain was attached to the hook and I was led back and forth through the city, presented to my people as a powerless prisoner. If I ever moved too slowly, or failed to obey any of the shouted instructions to bow or kneel, the chain was tugged until I did as I was told. I could feel my nose being torn apart and knew that soon the hook would be wrenched free.

The Assyrian commander walked with me and clearly enjoyed my suffering. So did the executioner who had done the work and still kept an eye on me. I knew that kind of man. I had used them myself, and now I was giving such a man pleasure. We returned to the temple court and the executioner examined me again, pulling the chain firmly to see what condition I was in. He decided that the hook might tear out, so they needed something

---

[24] http://freebibleimages.org/illustrations/king-manasseh/ Slide 13 (Sweet Publishing/FreeBibleimages.org, CC BY-SA 3.0 Unported)

else to control me. He took a larger hook and showed it to me in detail, explaining what was to happen. Then he pushed it through the bottom of my lower jaw and made sure it was fastened in place.

They led me away from Jerusalem as a mutilated prisoner, humiliated and ridiculed.

I knew that there was no hope. I had lost my throne and my kingdom, and nothing could ever restore them. In telling you my story, you must understand and believe this, or you will not learn the lesson I am trying so desperately to teach.

So let me say it again: I knew that there was no hope. None. And it was only in this situation that I finally began to realise that the gods I had worshipped could never help. I couldn't even believe in them myself. But now I was suffering exactly as the prophets of Yahweh had warned.

As we made our way to Babylon, where I was to be displayed as yet another king who had been defeated by Assyria, I began to think. My nose and jaw slowly healed as much as they could, but the chains were still used to control me as necessary. The chains and manacles of bronze that weighed down my hands and my feet ensured extra discomfort and made sure that I could never forget what had happened.

Slowly, I started to think. My life had been long and luxurious, and this was probably the only way to get me to review and reconsider. My prophets had not warned me of any of this. My soothsayers had not told me any news, and none of the dead people whom I had supposedly spoken to had whispered a word of it in the dark séances I had enjoyed.

None of the gods I had worshipped had known anything about this, or if they had known, they had not cared to warn me. The only one who had was the very God I had loathed and persecuted.

It took me several weeks to finally come to this conclusion and to honestly admit that I had been completely wrong in choosing who I would worship. Utter hopelessness accompanied this realisation. I recited in my mind the catalogue of my wrongs, gradually expanding it until I could no longer bear the magnitude of my crimes. Thousands – it had to be at least thousands, maybe hundreds of thousands – of people more righteous than I had died at my hand. Members of my own family, members of my court, gatekeepers, soldiers, guards, prophets, priests, scribes, shepherds, carpenters, stonemasons, builders, and so many others. I imagined mediums bringing all of those dead men to me, imagined all the dead attacking me and dragging me into the place of the dead to suffer with them. When one has imagined for decades that the dead still have voices and power, a guilty conscience like mine leads to terrors in the night.

If I had been left alone at any time during that journey, I would have ended my life with thankfulness. Guilt made life completely unbearable, and there was nothing I could do about it. Nothing could bring back the people I had killed, nothing could repair the damage my reign had done to the entire nation. Continuing life was impossible to contemplate.

Then from somewhere came memories of what many prophets of Yahweh had said to me – often their last words before I had them executed. They had spoken of repentance and claimed that Yahweh was a forgiving

God, even toward someone like me. Naturally, I couldn't suddenly rise from such depths of guilt to ecstatic happiness in the certainty that I had been forgiven. It was weeks longer before I could even begin to wonder if repentance might really be possible. There was no doubt that I was sorry. No doubt that I was certain I had done wrong. But hadn't I done too much wrong for forgiveness to be possible?

It was not until we arrived in Babylon after three months of travelling that I finally decided to take my sorrow and repentance before Yahweh. All of the other gods I had completely repudiated. Only Yahweh seemed worthy of worship. I knew nothing about prayer except for the prayers I had heard from my father when I was very young, and in the lowest of all possible situations, I tried to pray and acknowledge Yahweh as the one true God. I knew, or thought I knew, that I could never do anything to remedy what I had done. But I did want to admit that Yahweh was true and powerful.

That is where the miracle comes in. This is where you must learn a lesson from me about the forgiveness and inexpressible kindness of Yahweh. Assyria never allows its captive kings to return to their kingdoms. I returned to Jerusalem. Assyria never allows a kingdom it has once conquered to have freedom again. I returned to Jerusalem as king of an independent Judah, answerable only to Yahweh.

Can you see how utterly impossible that was?

Can you see how I can never again have any doubts that Yahweh is God and there is no other god beside him?

I returned to Jerusalem and sat again on my throne. My nose and jaw are permanent reminders of my time as a captive. The rest of my life is dedicated to trying to fix the wrongs I did. But some things, I will never be able to fix. More than 40 years of concentrated evil can't be overcome in just the few years I may have left. I think my son Amon is already beyond help. I try, but he reminds me of myself and the way I responded to my father. My grandson Josiah is different and I have high hopes for him. He is a godly child and I hope he will grow up to become a godly man and a godly king. Maybe he will be able to overcome all the evil that I did. I hope so.

I, Manasseh, am once again king over Judah in Jerusalem. This is irrefutable proof that Yahweh, the God of Judah, is in control of the nations. Listen to me and learn from me. Wrong can only be righted to some extent. The only way to truly fix wrong is never to do it. But if you have done wrong, I urge you now – repent! God does forgive. He even forgave me.

Ten

Have a Drink

For the true story, see Jeremiah 35.

One by one, they walked into the room while Jeremiah the prophet held the door open for them. He had invited them all to come to this particular chamber in the temple of Yahweh and they had all come – but not without some hesitation. Jeremiah was known for his prophecies of doom and his outspoken criticism of false worship. None of the family elders had welcomed the invitation.

It was Jaazaniah, the leader of the family, who had received the unexpected visitor. While sitting in his tent in a crowded courtyard in the western extension of the city, he had heard someone outside call his name. The family had not been in Jerusalem long and few people knew his name, so he had hurried out to see who was calling him. To own the truth, he had been a little concerned that it might be officers of the king or the governor of the city. Jerusalem was not a happy place, as the king's men enforced their own brand of justice. There were too many stories about innocent people disappearing and screams in the night which the neighbours were afraid to investigate.

The city was very crowded with people fleeing the attacks of Syrian and Babylonian raiding parties. And now Nebuchadnezzar's army had attacked the land and a siege was expected any day.

Jaazaniah and his family still lived in tents despite their move to the city, and it felt a little insecure at night. Sometimes they wondered whether they had done the right thing in coming into the city, but surely they would be safer in the capital of Judah than living unprotected at the mercy of Nebuchadnezzar and his armies?

All things considered, it was with relief that Jaazaniah saw an unarmed man of about average height, with a thick, dark beard, greying slightly at the edges, and eyes that looked kind but determined. His clothing looked well and truly in the common style of Judah, which convinced Jaazaniah that this was no representative of the king or nobles. King Jehoiakim and his men all wore expensive foreign clothes and were normally accompanied by armed guards who were quick to use their weapons on the slightest pretext.

Jerusalem was a city in which you had to be careful.

"I'm Jeremiah, the son of Hilkiah," announced the stranger. "Are you Jaazaniah, the son of Jeremiah?"

"Yes, that is my name," Jaazaniah replied, and waited to hear the stranger's business.

"I am here to invite you and your family to come to the temple of God about an important matter."

"My family?" repeated Jaazaniah, slowly. "There are many in my family. Who do you mean?"

Jeremiah smiled and waved his arms to encompass the collection of tents in the courtyard. "Any of your adult male relatives who live in these tents. The whole house of the Rechabites," he said.[25]

"I see," said Jaazaniah carefully, still wanting to find out why this prophet wanted them to go with him to the temple. Everyone had heard of Jeremiah, but not many had a good word to say about him. Many said he was a traitor, more interested in the other nations than in his own people.

"Can you come now?" asked Jeremiah, persistently.

"Not right now," said Jaazaniah, trying to buy time. "Some of my brothers are not here at present."

"Alright," said Jeremiah, "I can come back tomorrow afternoon at about the same time. Can you make sure that everyone will be here then?"

"I suppose I can, if you really want us to come."

"I do," confirmed Jeremiah.

The conversation had ended there and Jeremiah had left.

That evening, Jaazaniah had recounted the events to his brothers and other relatives, repeating Jeremiah's invitation to accompany him to the temple.

"Was it an invitation or a demand?" asked one of his brothers.

---

[25] Jeremiah 35:3 lists only men and does not make it clear whether women and children were included in the expression "and the whole house of the Rechabites". Taken in conjunction with Jeremiah 35:8 and the indication that this was just a chamber in the temple, it appears more likely that it would only have been men – or there would have been too many people to fit in the space available.

"It was worded as an invitation," replied Jaazaniah, "but it felt like a command."

"Should we go?" asked another brother.

"I don't want to," said a third.

"Nor do I," agreed Jaazaniah, "but I'm not sure that I dare refuse the demands of a prophet of Yahweh!"

"Yes, but why would he want to see us?" responded the third. "Do you think he could have heard of the weird rules of our ancestor?"

After much discussion, the men had grudgingly agreed that when Jeremiah came the next day, they would all be ready to go with him to the temple.

So it was that a nervous group of men had been waiting in their tents the next afternoon when Jeremiah arrived. Several had tried asking him what it was all about, but he had answered every question with the advice to wait until they were all in the temple, because he had something special for them there. They had looked at each other doubtfully, but finally followed him tentatively all the way to the temple, up the stairs and along a passageway to the door of the chamber of the sons of Hanan.

Jeremiah had opened the door and now he stood waiting as they filed into the room. "Each of you find a place to sit," he encouraged them, and they obediently arranged themselves on the seats that lined the walls of the chamber. An empty table sat in the middle of the room.

As soon as everyone was seated, Jeremiah said, "I'll be back soon," and left them waiting awkwardly.

After a short time, he returned carrying a large tray that was obviously heavy and held two large jugs, as well as many cups. Jeremiah thankfully placed the heavily-laden tray on the table and began to distribute the cups. The men exchanged glances, looking rather troubled. But Jeremiah smiled encouragingly as he gave each man his cup.

Jug and cups[26]

Once the distribution was complete, Jeremiah picked up one of the jugs and walked towards Jaazaniah. Every eye in the room was fixed worriedly on that jug. No-one could tell what was inside, and so much depended on what it was. The whole situation felt unreal to the Rechabites, and Jaazaniah put his hand over his cup as Jeremiah approached. He felt uncertain and uncomfortable – but he wasn't going to give up the restriction that he had cherished all his life. The ancient rule had certainly caused him trouble at times, but he was committed to it; it was worthwhile.

---

[26] "Set" by genma (openclipart:
https://openclipart.org/detail/243985/set)

"Drink wine!" said Jeremiah enthusiastically, holding up the pitcher. Most of the men in the room gasped – here was a prophet of God giving them an order which they could not obey. But did they dare to disobey? History told of some terrible things that had happened to people who disobeyed prophets!

Nobody breathed as the men waited to see what Jaazaniah would do.

"No, we can't," said Jaazaniah, firmly.

"But why not?" asked Jeremiah, looking surprised.

"We will drink no wine," answered Jaazaniah, "for Jonadab the son of Rechab, our father, commanded us, 'You shall not drink wine, neither you nor your sons forever. You shall not build a house; you shall not sow seed; you shall not plant or have a vineyard; but you shall live in tents all your days, that you may live many days in the land where you sojourn.' "

God's prophet stood and listened, still holding the pitcher of wine.

The next oldest brother continued earnestly: "We have obeyed the voice of Jonadab the son of Rechab, our father, in all that he commanded us, to drink no wine all our days, ourselves, our wives, our sons, or our daughters, and not to build houses to dwell in. We have no vineyard or field or seed, but we have lived in tents and have obeyed and done all that Jonadab our father commanded us."

"Then what has brought you to Jerusalem?" questioned Jeremiah.

"When Nebuchadnezzar king of Babylon came up against the land, we said, 'Come, and let us go to Jerusalem for fear of the army of the Chaldeans and the army of the Syrians.' So we are living in Jerusalem," explained Jaazaniah.

"I understand," said Jeremiah, but then, suddenly, a strangely intent look spread across his face and he said no more for a few moments as he seemed to look into the distance, seeing or hearing something that no-one else in the room could see or hear. Then, just as suddenly as the expression had spread over his face, it passed away again, and he continued, "God has told me to go and speak to the people of Judah and Jerusalem using you Rechabites as an example. God is pleased that you have obeyed your ancestor Jonadab, but disgusted that his people will not treat him with the same respect – although he has spoken to them again and again through many prophets."

"You mean that we don't have to drink this wine?" asked Jaazaniah, thankfully.

"No," said Jeremiah, and smiled again as all the men looked relieved. "God was just using the wine to demonstrate your faithfulness to the commands of your forefather. Thus says the Lord of hosts, the God of Israel: Because you have obeyed the command of Jonadab your father and kept all his precepts and done all that he commanded you, therefore thus says the Lord of hosts, the God of Israel: 'Jonadab the son of Rechab shall never lack a man to stand before me.' "

Eleven

Is my Husband Going Mad?

For the true story, see Ezekiel 1-5 and 24:15-27.

My husband, Ezekiel, is a wonderful, Godly man whom I admire hugely and who cares for me delightfully. I have never had any doubts that he loves me or that I am "the delight of his eyes", as he so frequently says – or writes, nowadays.

However, I am concerned about him.

Ten years ago, when we lived in Judah, there was no problem. We were both young when we were married, and Ezekiel was only 25 years old when King Nebuchadnezzar of Babylon took us, and thousands of others, into captivity, along with our king Jehoiachin. King Jehoiachin was even younger than me – only 18 years old – and had been king for a mere 3 months and 10 days.

Once we got used to captivity, everything was fine. But Ezekiel comes from a priestly family, and he would have become a priest when he turned 30 if we had been in Jerusalem. Instead, by that time we had been in Babylon for five years.

Maybe it was missing the opportunity to follow his ancestral career that put him under stress. Anyway, whatever it was, the year he turned 30 was the start of his strange behaviour.

In fact, I can even tie it down to one particular day: the fifth day of the fourth month in the fifth year of our captivity. Until then, he was growing in godliness in an admirable way. I have no doubt that he was coming closer and closer to Yahweh our God, but on that day, something happened.

Ezekiel has explained to me what happened from his point of view, but it seems utterly incredible. Of course, I completely believed him when he told me that this was what he had seen, but I couldn't help wondering whether it was more delusion than vision. If only I could have seen it myself, there wouldn't be any question: we could have shared the same weird experiences and our neighbours would be free to consider us both mad!

Ezekiel saw four living creatures and wheels[27]

Anyway, he told me that he saw a stormy wind coming from the north with brightness and some strange living things with four faces and four wings and strange shapes, looking like burning coals and moving very quickly – almost looking like lightning in their speed. Not only that, but each living creature had a very strange thing that Ezekiel said stayed right near it wherever it moved, something that looked to him like a wheel within a wheel, though I'm not really sure what that means. When he told me, I'm afraid my first response was that it probably meant that he needed more sleep!

I really didn't know what to think. Ezekiel has always been very sensible and down-to-earth, and he still looked and sounded just the same as he described what he had seen. He didn't suddenly look wild-eyed or over-stressed. He just looked like Ezekiel, but what he said didn't fit with anything that happens in ordinary life. He also told me that he saw a throne and something that looked quite human sitting on the throne – except that it looked like it was made of hot metal and glowed with light and fire.

If your husband or wife, or maybe your son or daughter, told you that they had seen something like that, wouldn't you be doubtful? Of course, my Ezekiel had always been steady and reliable, so naturally, I tried hard to believe him, but really, was it possible?

There was also more, much more, about how he knew that it was the glory of God and that something spoke to him and told him that he was being sent to the people of Israel as a prophet. Well, I heard Jeremiah the prophet speaking in Jerusalem before we were brought into captivity, and he never spoke about strange creatures like lightning or wheels within wheels. He just spoke simple messages and warnings from God – things that could be understood, and warnings about things that have happened, too.

If God had just given Ezekiel nice, straightforward messages, things like Jeremiah said, I would have been pleased, even proud of him. But trying to cope with a husband who talks about cherubim and wheels and thrones in the sky has been very difficult.

Next, he was given a scroll to eat. How was I meant to explain that to my family and our neighbours?

We talked about it and he explained to me that God had told him to speak to the people who are here in captivity with us. The scroll had had all sorts of terrible woes written on it, and I gathered that my husband didn't want to say them to the people. He told me that God had warned him not to be stubborn like the rest of the people are, but after that episode he didn't do anything for a week. Every day, he just sat there and did nothing. No speaking, no doing, nothing at all. I sensed that he was angry, although he didn't explain it to me. Maybe he was upset that God had sent us all into captivity, but still planned to punish us more. Maybe my husband didn't think that was fair. I really don't know, and that's part of the problem. He didn't tell me everything at the time; and now he can't.

If God really was telling him to say something, this sitting around in silence was not the way to please God.

Maybe he would have obeyed God sooner if I had been a bit quicker to believe everything that he told me. Whatever the reason, at the end of that week he stopped talking completely. And in the years since then, he hasn't said a word unless he had some specific message to deliver directly from God.

Now, once again I ask: if all this had happened to your husband or wife, what would you think? Would you wonder whether he or she was going crazy? Or would you rejoice that God was clearly speaking to them?

I'm so mixed up about it all. I want to believe it, because Ezekiel has never lied to me or shown any signs of mental instability, but it is so different from anything I ever expected a prophet of God to do. Having faith in things that are so far from our common experience is very hard. I keep asking myself, "Why would God really do it this way?", and I can't find an answer I can be sure of.

Nevertheless, I still love and admire Ezekiel, so I do my best to believe him and support him.

But every time I think I can accept how things are, even stranger things happen.

When the next order came, Ezekiel wrote me a note to explain it all. He was to make a model of Jerusalem on a brick and put it on the ground. Then he had to lie down in front of it and act as if he was besieging the city.

A grown man! Acting like a child playing games! And not just for a short time either. He wrote that God had said that he was to lie on his left side "pressing the siege" for 390 days. Can you imagine the social shame of having a husband who lies on the ground in front of a brick for more than a year, shaking his fist at it and…oh, I can't go on. I just don't want to remember it. And as for the way he lost weight on the starvation rations God had allocated him, I can't imagine any wife being happy with that!

All of my neighbours were telling me that he was mad, and I couldn't even show my love for him by feeding him good, healthy meals.

And it has just kept on getting worse. I have had more than four years now of struggling with my own attitudes, as everyone around me agrees that Ezekiel has lost his mind.

I have watched him cutting off his hair with a sword and then throwing the hair up in the air and rushing around waving his sword as it falls to the ground.

I have talked to him, begging for some explanation or proof, only to have him point to his mouth to remind me that he cannot speak. Then God wants him to give a message to the people and suddenly he can speak clearly and loudly, and it's just like the old Ezekiel again, the strong, kind voice I loved to listen to in the good old days.

Do I believe him about all that God has done with him? Yes, I think I do. I certainly try to, but as a result, everybody says that I must be mad too!

And right now I am very concerned because I have not been well for the last few weeks. I don't seem to be getting any better – in fact, I may even be getting worse.

I can't look after him properly with the way I am, and today it has occurred to me for the first time to wonder: What will happen to him if I die? Nobody else will look after him properly. They all think he is mad.

A few times today, I have caught him looking at me in a way I can't quite describe, almost as if something terrible is about to happen.

Oh, Ezekiel, may God care for you if I cannot.

Historical note:

Ezekiel's wife died on the tenth day of the tenth month in the ninth year of their captivity. On the morning of that day, God warned him what was about to happen, and in the evening, the "delight of his eyes" died. However, God did care for him, and three years later he regained his voice (Ezekiel 33:21-22). After that, his work as a prophet continued for many years.

Part Two: New Testament

Twelve

A Shepherd's Story

For the true story, see Luke 2.

My father was a shepherd, as was his father before him. I'm told that there have been shepherds in our family ever since the people of Israel returned from captivity in Babylon.

I love my sheep, and a life in the open air is as necessary to me as eating – although we often freeze at night and melt during the day! But when I lie on the ground at night and look up at the stars it feels as though they might almost swallow me up with their beauty. At times, I feel dizzy with the slow-moving panorama.

Yet it is not only the sky that satisfies my desire for beauty, and, after all, the beauty of the sky is a cold and silent sort of beauty, breathtaking though it is. But the creation around me is close at hand, and its sounds and sights warm my heart daily as the years wax and wane. Eager growth fills each spring, while summer and autumn consolidate the growth and maturity brings food for all from the hand of God. Even the quiet death of winter has a beauty all of its own.

Every season and each new moon shows the handiwork of Yahweh our God, and I am blessed to have a job which allows me to be more a part of it than most.

Of course, we don't always appreciate God's work as we should, and frigid nights bring volleys of selfish complaints from me as much as from the next man. Nevertheless, most earn their livelihood far from the trees and flowers, the breezes and stillness that fill my days with wonder.

I really don't want to sound as if I am some sort of wise and holy man who sees everything clearly. I am just a simple shepherd whose job is to care for generations of loveable – but often foolish – sheep that provide wool and meat and leather for us all. For me, they also provide noisy and often demanding companionship and teach me many lessons in life.

Much of the time, my life is leisurely, as I slowly lead the flocks from place to place to feed on the sparse pastures of Judea. The lifespan of a sheep is short enough that I can watch generations come and go: the wise and the simple, the innocent and the crafty. Some sheep learn from me as their shepherd, while others struggle against me at every step and will never believe that I really do have their best interests at heart. Some try to hide their every action from me and stumble into trouble at every turn, while just a few seem to really like my company and appreciate it when they notice me doing something for them.

Being a shepherd has taught me a lot about how God must view people. King David was the most famous of all shepherds, and God took him to be shepherd of his people. I couldn't cope with shepherding people – they are even more stubborn than sheep, and every bit as thoughtless!

Once I had a ewe who seemed to have no idea of how to be a mother. When she was young, she would give birth and then wander off, leaving her lamb or lambs uncared-for. We found her first lamb wandering in all sorts of places – normally with its mother being nowhere in sight. Over time, we managed to convince her to show at least a basic level of care for her young, but she always seemed to fight against it. She was a very selfish and argumentative ewe, even into her old age. But she did learn the most important lessons – otherwise, I would have needed to get rid of her earlier.

Some humans, however, never will learn. Take Herod, for example. Like that ewe, he has no natural care for his family. To him, children are a nuisance, and once they reach adulthood they are likely to be competition. Unfortunately, nobody has ever been able to teach him the basics of family love, so he just ignores them – unless he begins to fear that they are a threat to his position. If that happens, he kills them. Our ewe never did anything so cruel as that.

Some call Herod, "Herod the Great", but it's not because he is a great person. If the name reflected his personality, it would be Herod the Brutal Paranoid.

Anyway, the tale that I want to tell you now involves shepherds and babies, and it has a very sad ending – brought about directly by Herod.

Judea is part of the Roman Empire, and the emperor in far-off Rome wanted to make sure that we were all paying our taxes, so he ordered everyone to return to their ancestral home to be counted. For most people around here, including me, this wasn't a problem, because most of us don't move very far from the land inherited from our fathers. Our laws of ownership and inheritance make it much easier to stay put than to move – unless one wants to live in a city, which I just can't imagine!

I am from the tribe of Judah and my family's land is near Bethlehem, the town famous as the city of King David. We farm the land to produce most of our own food, but shepherd our sheep to earn extra money. The sheep that we keep from year to year produce wool, but we also sell some sheep as meat or for sacrifices in the temple.

So we do some farming, but I would call myself a shepherd, not a farmer. That is the work I love.

There was nothing to suggest that this night was anything special. With night falling as usual, a few of us shepherds had gathered together at dusk at a sheepfold with our flocks. Such folds are dotted around the hills in the area, common property, with stone walls built and maintained by generations of shepherds. They are generally located in open areas where the soil is not good enough for farming, but tufts of good grass provide enough food for our sheep, as long as we keep moving around.

It is a lifestyle that keeps us cut off from the life of cities and towns, where work ends at sunset and men sleep in safety behind walls and gates. For us, nights are often times of interrupted sleep, times when a trained instinct can trigger sudden watchfulness lest swift danger should erupt from behind a shadowy rock. Yet many other nights meander quietly from dusk to dawn without any unpleasant interruptions.

Shepherds were out in the fields[28]

On this night, there was nothing to indicate that something special was coming. Even when we discussed it later, none of us could remember anything different about the sunset or the evening breezes. There was nothing to make the night distinctive as we each settled our sheep for the night and cooked our evening meal. The fire had been made ready for the night too, large enough to deter wild animals but not so bright as to ruin the night vision of the watchman. Shepherds and sheep had all fallen asleep, leaving a single watchman alone to contemplate the chill of the night and the cold clear stars that shone above.

I was the watchman that night.

An hour passed and the moon had risen. Then, without any warning, suddenly a brighter light spread over the scene. Now from time to time we shepherds do see things like this, bright lights in the sky, and even what some people call "shooting stars". Sometimes they last for a few seconds, and once I even saw one that swept across the sky and then exploded into pieces that lit up the countryside like daylight.

But this was different. The light grew steadily and seemed to be everywhere around me. For a while, it didn't even occur to me to wake the other shepherds – I just sat and gazed around in wonder as the trees and shrubs nearby were lit with this strange, ever-strengthening glow.

Then the sheep began to stir, and one or two of them bleated with the surprised sound that sheep sometimes have. The noise disturbed other sheep, who added their bleating to the rapidly increasing clamour, and after that there was no need for me to wake up the other shepherds – they were all awake. Some asked what was going on, while others merely watched silently, taking in the ethereal beauty of the scene. But there was fear too, I can tell you. I'm not young, and nothing like this had ever happened before in my lifetime, nor those of the older shepherds either. Soon the light was bright enough to make the moon look dim, and then, in a terrifying instant, I suddenly saw where the light was coming from. An angel – it must have been an angel, for ordinary men don't shine like that – came around the corner of the sheepfold and walked towards me as I sat at the entrance.

My heart stood still and I stopped breathing as panic gripped me. The fear that I felt was greater than any I had ever experienced when facing wild animals, or even that time when lightning struck a tree very close to me.

And then he spoke, saying, "Don't be afraid, for I bring you good news." At the time, it didn't even occur to me to wonder why an angel would come and speak to a group of shepherds in the middle of the night, though I've wondered since why we were chosen. What good news could possibly deserve such a strange event?

Some people say that there are angels around us all the time, but I had never seen one before and I was terrified. And being told not to be afraid didn't seem to help very much either. I was so afraid that I could neither stand nor speak; I just sat there and quivered as the angel approached.

"I bring you good news of great joy that will be for all the people," continued the angel, speaking to me and to all of the other shepherds inside the fold. "For unto you is born this day in the city of David a Saviour, who is Christ the Lord. And this will be a sign for you: you will find a baby wrapped in swaddling cloths and lying in a manger."

There was no time to digest his words, because suddenly, all around and above the angel was an enormous crowd of other angels. The night exploded with light and sound as this heavenly army, standing on the ground around the angel or floating above it wherever they happened to be, praised God and said, "Glory to God in the highest, and on earth peace among those with whom he is pleased!"

Some spoke, some sang, and some shouted, but all praised God, filling the hillside air with joyous celebration. Light and happiness had come to the earth in a way never seen before. This continued for some time, but I don't have any idea how long. Finally, as we watched, all of the angels went away, ascending into the sky in a shining, glorious throng, shrinking in the distance above until they dwindled to a point of light and disappeared.

But though the darkness had returned, I can't say the same about the silence, because none of us could keep quiet about what we had just seen. Some commented on the beauty of the voices, some on the brightness of the light, and still others on the clothing of the angels. After a time, though, we finally started to talk about what we had been told. Good news. Great joy. A saviour, the Christ. Someone pointed out that the city of David must be Bethlehem, such a short distance away. Now Bethlehem is not a large town, and one way or another, we knew of all of the babies that were due to be born soon. No-one could think of any expectant mother in Bethlehem who could possibly have given birth to the Messiah. But then someone suggested that it could be one of the visitors who had come to register in the census, and another man remembered that he had seen a young woman among the visitors in Bethlehem who was clearly expecting a baby very soon.

"Let's go over to Bethlehem and see this baby," I said, willing to go by myself if I had to, but preferring to have company if possible.

"Yes, let's go and see what has happened," answered one of the other shepherds, "since God has specially told us about it."

"But we can't leave the sheep here," objected another.

"Of course we can," I replied. "Just make sure the entrance is blocked, and then let's hurry."

So we hurried. The moon made it easy to find our way to Bethlehem, but when we got there, it wasn't quite so easy, since we didn't know exactly where to go. First, we all went to one of the inns to see whether the baby was there. It wasn't, but the innkeeper spoke of a young couple who had been expecting a baby, due any time. "They found a place to stay," he said reassuringly, then laughed a little as he continued, "but if the baby has been born, it has probably ended up in a manger!"

That was just what we were looking for, since, when we came to think of it, that was what the angel had said too; so we quickly went to the place. We found exactly what the angel had said: a baby wrapped in swaddling cloths and lying in a manger. Our arrival was obviously a bit of a surprise to the father – a young man called Joseph – and we found out from him that he was indeed descended from the line of King David. In fact, if he has his facts right, he would probably be first in line for the kingship if only we could get rid of Herod and the Romans.

Now, I believe strongly in God. I offer my sacrifices at the temple, and I pray to God often – but this was all a bit too uncanny for me!

This baby was to be a saviour. Now, there is no doubt that Israel needs a saviour, but can a baby do the job? And angels had appeared to tell a group of shepherds about the birth of a baby: why would God do that? Why not tell Herod instead, and force him to let this baby be king? Let Herod know that a baby had been born to just the right man that very day, and let him check it out. But then again, when a monster like Herod is in control, announcing the birth of a baby is just going to get the baby killed.

Unfortunately, that was the horrible truth of the matter; the terrible outcome.

As we hurried back to our sheep later that night, we couldn't stop talking about the amazing events. I even went to look at the place where the angel had stood to speak to us, but there was no trace of anything special. All that we had to work on was our memories and our shared experience. We told everyone we could, and everyone was amazed, although the religious leaders were rather sceptical about the idea that God would deliver a message like that to shepherds rather than to experts in the law or priests.

I didn't go and visit the couple again, but I heard that they had stayed in Bethlehem and moved into a house of their own.

Well, the news of the baby spread, particularly when some wise men also visited a few months later – of course, people listened to them more than they listened to us. Unfortunately, though, they had stopped at Jerusalem first to make enquiries about a new king, and that was what really let the cat out of the bag. As I said, Herod was never one to let a potential competitor survive.

∝

Sadly, it was a tragic end to a beautiful story. Having heard of the child from the wise men, a while later Herod ordered his soldiers to go and kill every young boy in and around Bethlehem. The soldiers did what they were told, and every boy two years old and under was slaughtered, leaving many heartbroken families mourning their loss.

But one baby boy was more important than all of the others, and now even his parents have disappeared – probably having withdrawn to mourn his tragic loss. Did we shepherds help to cause his death by telling everyone what the angel had said to us?

I suppose God will have to try sending another saviour – unless the child somehow escaped Herod's killing squads. But I don't think there's much hope of that…

Thirteen

A Touch of Faith

For the true story, see Matthew 9:19-22; Mark 5:25-34; Luke 8:43-48.

Twelve long years of being unclean. When I think back on it now, it seems like an unbearable time, and I'm amazed that I survived it. No thanks for that can go to the many different doctors I saw: they didn't heal me at all; instead, I kept getting ever so slowly worse.

Hundreds of years ago, there was a king of Judah who was afflicted by a disease in his feet as he grew old.[29] He suffered terribly and looked for doctors to heal him, but nothing helped. Our scriptures describe his search for a medical solution in a way that shows that it was not the best answer, saying that "even in his disease he did not seek the Lord, but sought help from physicians." Well, that was the same with me for all of those twelve years. When my problem started, I found a doctor and hoped that he could cure me. He couldn't, but he could take my money. Oh, yes. He was good at that. After a while, I looked for another doctor to see whether he could do

---

[29] 2 Chronicles 16:12; 1 Kings 15:23

better. Unfortunately, the only thing he did better was taking my money. Over the years I tried many more doctors, but just like with King Asa, my quest failed. King Asa died with his problem, and it looked as if I would do the same with mine.

Scripture is written to help us to learn. Examples from the lives of all sorts of people are intended to help us to learn about God's wishes. But when you are unclean, nobody wants you around in synagogues or any other assembly of the people. At our synagogues we have readings from scripture, but they could not help me. In Jerusalem we have priests and experts in the law, but not for me – no-one would even talk to me. Instead, I was left on my own, trusting human doctors rather than God, spending all of my money and gradually getting sicker.

Ironic, isn't it, that someone who could have learned from the example of King Asa was never able to hear it? God has provided guidance and help, but the very people who need to hear them most cannot do so! It's only now that I am clean again that I have been able to hear this example read in the synagogue. I wonder how many others have missed out on words of God that they needed because of being unclean? Of course, this is not God's fault. Others could have told me, but did not – for whatever reason. Maybe I should have been asking more.

When you are unclean because of a discharge or bleeding, whether you are a man or a woman, you cannot interact ordinarily with other people. Anyone you touch, or anyone who touches you, becomes unclean. Any bed you lie on, any seat you sit on, is made unclean. Ordinary life is utterly impossible. This curse I had suffered for 12 years.

Many people had been cured by Jesus, so he was always surrounded by people who wanted to be cured. People in front of him, people behind him, people crowding around everywhere. So what could I do? If I tried to go to Jesus and let people know that I was unclean, everyone would tell me to go away and refuse to let me anywhere near. Believe me, I know – it happened all the time near my home.

Yet if I joined the throng without warning anyone, I would be touching many people and making them all unclean. Even if they didn't know it, God would.

What should I do? I could keep spending what little money I had left on doctors and getting slowly worse, or I could try to get close to Jesus.

I made up my mind that I had to go and see Jesus, but I hadn't worked out how I would manage it.

Stories about Jesus were spreading all over the countryside, but there was one that got my attention more than any of the others. People spoke of a leper who had approached Jesus and said, "If you are willing, you can make me clean."

It was just as simple as that, and Jesus' reply had been just as simple: "I am willing, be clean." Then he touched the man and he was cured of his leprosy.

So much better than my visits to doctors! They always want to know my medical history, how long the problem has lasted, how weak I feel, how many other doctors I have seen, what medicines have been tried, and so many, many more questions. But Jesus didn't need to know any of that – he just cured people. It almost makes me feel sorry for doctors!

Apparently Jesus had had just two more things to say to that man: he forbade him from telling anyone what had happened and he told him to go to the priest and offer the sacrifice required for his cleansing. I don't know about the cleansing, but from what I hear, the man has never breathed a word to anyone about his healing – the reports have spread from other witnesses. Being unable to tell people how he had been healed must have made things very difficult for him. Old friends who had met him would have asked, "How did you get cured?" I couldn't imagine what sort of answer one might give. Could it be: "I can't tell you that" or "It doesn't matter, what matters is that I am better"? I knew that if I was successful in my goal, I might have to work out such an answer myself.

I hoped so.

Finally, one day news came that Jesus was in town, and I made up my mind to do something. I still had no firm plans, but I was determined to go to Jesus and see what happened. By that time I was sure that Jesus could heal me, and would be willing to. The only question was how to give him the chance.

When I arrived at the place where Jesus was, it wasn't hard to tell that he was there, although I couldn't see him. The crowds were even worse than I had imagined they might be. As I approached Jesus, I couldn't see what was going on, but I heard that a leader of the synagogue was kneeling before Jesus, begging him to go with him to heal his daughter. Then Jesus stood and followed him, with his disciples, and I could see him.

Oh, what should I do? This visit could take some time, and if I stayed in the crowd close to Jesus for too long, someone might recognise me.

I was in a torment of uncertainty. Should I join the crowd and ignore my uncleanness? Or would it be best to go back home and wait until tomorrow?

In the end, I decided to join the crowd and see whether an opportunity would arise on the way to the leader's house. I just couldn't wait. As the crowd moved, still packed close around Jesus, I gradually worked my way through it. You will have to believe me in this, but I really did do the best I could to avoid touching people. However, I confess that I did brush against some people. I was in such a state that you can't really imagine what it was like. I should have stopped and let the crowd pass, but I couldn't. I know that was wrong. I had always tried to avoid making others unclean in my affliction, but I failed badly on that day.

Eventually I was close enough to Jesus that I could almost touch him, but not quite. I was off to his left and a short way behind, when suddenly the crowd stopped for some reason – you know what crowds are like. I still couldn't quite reach him, but it occurred to me that if I bent down and stretched out my arm past people's legs, I could probably just reach the edge of his cloak. So I bobbed down and looked through the sea of legs and clothes, quickly identifying Jesus' legs and his garment with the tassels on the corners including the blue thread that the law required. I reached out desperately, right as the crowd started to move, and just – only just – managed to touch his cloak.

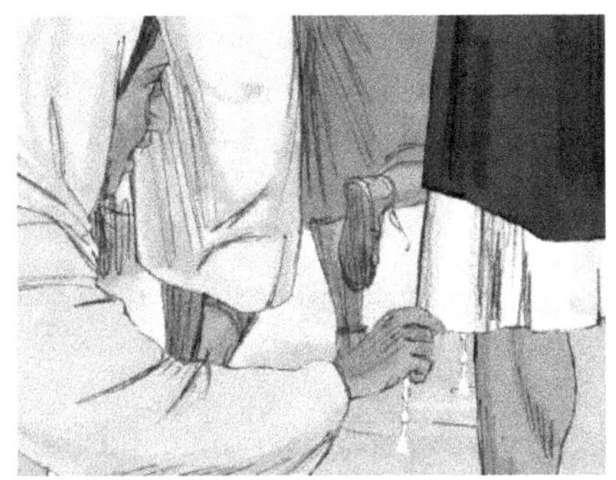

The woman reached out and touched the edge of Jesus' garment[30]

The response was amazing. I knew instantly that my bleeding had stopped. As quickly as I could, I pulled back my hand and stood up again, all in one fluid movement.

That was my experience of the encounter, but apparently Jesus too had been able to feel the power that had stopped my bleeding. Straight away, he stopped and turned, looking around and asking, "Who touched my clothes?" Oh, it was frightening. My euphoria at having been cured suddenly became terror. I dreaded being caught.

I wasn't next to him, so there was still a chance that I wouldn't be caught. I started trying to edge away, but Jesus' reaction and his words had caused the crowd to pack itself even more tightly around him. There was no escape.

Jesus was looking around at the crowd, and everyone he looked at said quickly, "It wasn't me."

---

[30] http://freebibleimages.org/illustrations/jairus-daughter/ Slide 7 (Sweet Publishing/FreeBibleimages.org, CC BY-SA 3.0 Unported)

Peter, one of his disciples, said to him, "Master, the crowds are all around you and pressing on you!"

Jesus' voice wasn't harsh or angry as he replied, but it was insistent: "Someone touched me, for I know that power has gone out from me."

All of the people right next to Jesus had denied touching him, and now he was looking further afield… looking at me.

I suppose it was my feeling of guilt at having made people unclean that made me so frightened, but I spoke to him anyway: "It was me," I said, my voice shaking. "I have been bleeding for twelve years, and no doctor can heal me, so I came and touched just the edge of your cloak, just the tassel, and now I am healed. I knew that you could heal me, so I didn't need to talk to you, but I am sorry… my uncleanness…"

My words stumbled to a halt and I looked pleadingly at him. Jesus smiled at me and encouraged me. He told me that my faith had made me well. As soon as he said it, I knew that it was true. I had never doubted that he could heal me. What a wonderful man, to inspire such faith in a sick woman!

There was just one more step which I hadn't even realised was needed. I had felt wonderful after one simple touch of his garment, but then Jesus said, "Go in peace and be healed of your disease," and suddenly I knew that an even greater healing had come upon me. I can't explain it any more than that, but I was fully, completely cured by Jesus' blessing – and filled with peace as well.

Fourteen

A Short Story

For the true story, see Luke 19:1-10.

Some people say that short people are more determined than tall people, because they always have to fight harder to get what they want. Small people can't reach as high, can't see over things as easily, and in many contexts, they won't get seen much either. Little people, they say, need to really make a lot of noise in life to get noticed.

Well, whether that is true or not I don't know. What I do know is that I am not very tall, but despite that, I got noticed when lots of other people didn't. And it completely changed my life.

My name is Zacchaeus and I am a chief tax collector, living in Jericho. I am also rich, but not as rich as I used to be.

Did you know that taxes make society? Roads, armies, security, law enforcement, government, public buildings and many other things come from the payment of taxes and duties. Furthermore, the income from taxes has to be reliable and consistent. If no taxes were received in any year, then the empire would collapse, with revolutions and uprisings everywhere.

So tax collection in the Roman empire was often contracted out after a tender process. Rich people would bid for the right to collect taxes in a country or smaller area. The winner had to pay the agreed amount each year to the government so that there would be no nasty surprises or bad years where the income did not meet expectations.

If they didn't collect enough tax each year, they lost money. But any extra they collected was theirs to keep – bumper crops, population increases or any other windfalls lined their pockets with gold, and so did any dubious practices they could get away with while collecting the taxes.

I didn't believe in that sort of thing.

Laws defined what was taxable and who had to pay taxes, and the bidders had to estimate how much they could collect based on population estimates and expectations of taxable events.

You might think that the calculations should be quite exact, but it doesn't work that easily – weather and disease can have a big impact on the tax that can be collected each year. Not only that, but people move to different places and the population isn't counted very often so estimates can be badly wrong at times.

Once a contract was agreed, a hierarchy of collectors would do the work of collecting the money from individuals, while the heavy weight of Roman law would make sure that the collectors were protected and supported. There was always money to be made for everyone in the tax hierarchy. If a farmer argued with a tax collector, Roman judges would be more likely to listen to the tax collector – after all, without the tax collectors, bureaucrats would not get paid. The power was all on the side of the tax collectors.

I was a chief tax collector. Being rich had bought me the job and doing the job made me richer still. Many tax collectors worked for me and the money they collected was much more than the money I had to pay each year.

If you listen to the ordinary citizens of Israel, you will get the picture that everyone involved in tax collecting is a traitor and a thief, no better than the thieves that prey on innocent travellers along a quiet road.

But it's really not that simple.

There are tax collectors who are dedicated servants of God. I was one of them and quite happy overall with how I was living. Rich? Yes, I was rich – so was Abraham. Working for the foreign overlords? Yes, I was, just as Daniel had. A rogue who cheats people out of money all the time? No, that's not me at all.

Some tax collectors are cheats, but I wasn't. Many won't believe me about this, but I hope you will.

As a chief tax collector, I had to assign areas for tax collectors to look after. Census details told me how many people lived in the area and the tax collector calculated how much money they should owe me after collecting the tax. Income tax, import and export taxes, crop taxes, sales tax, emergency taxes, property taxes and various others all had defined rates and had to be applied to the right people. That was a tax collector's job.

As you might expect, farmers did the best they could to avoid the crop taxes and property taxes, and sales taxes were hard to levy if you didn't arrive until after all the goods were sold – all the merchants reported that they had started with very few goods, hardly any at all. Everyone tried to avoid giving a tax collector even the smallest copper coins and the lies they told should have stuck in their throats. Some even came up with "religious" excuses to avoid the tax, claiming that no Israelites should pay taxes because Caesar was a foreigner and paying tax to him was being unfaithful to God. A conscience is a good thing, but a conscience blinded by the love of money is not.

Sometimes it made me wonder how people could complain about tax collectors being greedy or being cheats – all the rest of the people were trying to cheat me whenever they could! They were all pleased to have good roads for safe travel, but were far too greedy to want to pay for them.

But I kept going with my job, because the love of money was too strong in me also.

Anyway, if I didn't collect the taxes from my tax collectors, it didn't reduce the amount of money I had to give to my bosses. So I kept collecting, but I was as fair as I could be.

I didn't realise it at the time, but it is the love of money that makes tax collecting so attractive and so repugnant. Attractive to collectors and repugnant to those who must pay. I had not known just how much almost everything I did was driven by a love of money. My love of God was still there, but it was being strangled by my love of money. I knew that some people were short of food, but I made all sorts of excuses why I shouldn't give them the food they needed. I understood that there were people who did not have enough clothes, particularly when the cold winter nights traced the grass and leaves in delicate frost. Yet I would never give any of my spare clothes to them, although I had many sets of clothes which could have warmed them and their children when biting winds brought bitter cold. I was blind. Blinded by money. And I used my intellect to reason away the needs and excuse my selfish behaviour.

But still, I loved God, and finally that drove me to do something that actually opened my eyes.

I heard of Jesus and I went to listen to him. That was a good idea, but it didn't work. Too many people recognised me: no-one wanted me in the crowd, and no-one let me get near enough to hear Jesus speak. For the time being, I gave up, although I continued to find out more about him and his teachings.

It was money that strengthened my determination to see him, because I heard that Jesus lived almost completely without money. If people gave him food, he accepted it, but if people gave him money, it went straight to the poor. I had even heard an amazing rumour that he had been given some precious presents a little while after his birth, but that once he grew up, he had given the money away. I didn't know whether it was true or not, but it certainly got my attention.

On another occasion when Jesus came to Jericho, I joined the crowd and tried to see him. Once again, I had no chance, but this time I was more determined. I ran on ahead, through Jericho and out onto the road where it led up towards Jerusalem. There I found a tree and climbed into it, making sure that I couldn't be easily seen from below. I was afraid that if the crowd saw me and recognised who I was, they might throw things at me.

I sat there quietly and waited, hoping that I had guessed right and that Jesus would come this way immediately. It seemed to take an age, but eventually, I saw a crowd coming, with Jesus near the front. Big crowds move slowly, so I had to wait quite a while.

Finally, I could see Jesus and that was the first thing I had wanted to do. His face looked clear and honest and his voice rang out over the noise of the crowd as they bustled about him.

Then I got the shock of my life as he suddenly looked up at me, almost completely concealed by the branches and leaves of the thick tree I had chosen, and our eyes met. Straight away, I knew that he had seen me and I wondered what he would do. If he was so unaffected by money, would he despise me for my riches and strong attachment to money? For a moment I was terrified and wished I could escape – and maybe get rid of some of my money too.

An even greater shock was in store, because he called me by name: "Zacchaeus, hurry and come down, for I must stay at your house today."

At my house? That was so much more than I could ever have hoped for that I hurried so much that I almost fell out of the tree.

Zacchaeus climbs down from the tree[31]

I can't remember what I said to him, but we made our way to my house and Jesus came into the grand home I had spent so much money beautifying over the years. It was quite embarrassing having this holy man walking on the marble floors as the ornamental fountains tinkled in the background. He didn't seem upset or embarrassed, and he ignored the people who sneered at him for coming to the house of a tax collector.

We sat and talked and he opened up the scriptures to me. I have never heard anyone explain God's word so clearly. Never a word did he speak about the incongruity between his life and mine, his goals and mine.

But it made me feel that I needed to do something. I examined my heart and made sure that I could really fulfil the commitment I was about to make.

Finally I was sure and I asked Jesus if I could make an announcement to everyone. He told me that was a good idea, so I stood up.

"Behold, Lord," I said, making sure everyone else could hear as well. I wanted to be held accountable for this commitment. "The half of my goods I give to the poor. And if I have defrauded anyone of anything, I restore it fourfold."

I had a clear conscience about not having defrauded anyone, or else I couldn't have promised to give back four times the amount. It wouldn't have taken much cheating at all to quickly consume the half of my goods that I had not already promised to the poor. But I wanted to be a bit careful too. I needed to make sure that I could really do without my money. There was no point in making a grand commitment and falling at the first step. I thought I could do it, but I looked at Jesus to see if he was convinced.

It was such a glorious confirmation when he said, "Today salvation has come to this house, since he also is a son of Abraham. For the Son of Man came to seek and to save the lost."

Jesus was convinced, so I knew I could do it.

Fifteen

Has my Brother Gone Mad?

For the true story, see Mark 3:20-35. John 7:3-10 shows how Jesus' family felt about him at other times and John 10:20 shows that the idea of him being mad was not unique to his family.

Of all the people I have ever known, I would always have said that my brother Jesus[32] has the firmest possible grip on his sanity.

But just recently, I've begun to think we may have cause to question that.

When Jesus reached thirty years of age,[33] he left home and began to tell people all over the country that they should repent because the kingdom of heaven is near.

---

[32] This story assumes that the brothers and sisters of Jesus referred to in the New Testament (eg. Matthew 13:55-56; Mark 6:3; Acts 1:14; Galatians 1:19; 1 Corinthians 9:5) were half brothers and sisters who shared the same mother with Jesus (Mary), not the product of a previous marriage between Joseph and some other woman of whom there is no record. Mary was a virgin until the birth of Jesus (Matthew 1:24-25), but there is no suggestion in the Bible that this continued. In fact, the clear implication of Matthew 1:24-25 is otherwise.

[33] Luke 3:23

Many people think that sounds sort of crazy by itself, but it certainly didn't sound crazy when Jesus spoke about it. Everything that Jesus says makes perfect sense when he explains it, but when he's not there it can be harder to understand why he does some things.

I suppose I should tell you a bit about our background so that you will understand better what the family thinks of Jesus.

Jesus was conceived before our parents were married and that caused quite a bit of trouble for them. Our mother says that Jesus was conceived in her by the work of the Holy Spirit, not by any human father.

I believe her.

We children all grew up in Nazareth with Dad working as a carpenter and builder. He was a righteous man and the whole family was very religious and we went to the synagogue every Sabbath.

Jesus was an amazing brother to have. My other brothers were more or less like me, but Jesus was different. The rest of us all had our petty jealousies and sibling rivalries, but those things never came from him.

There were times when items were broken and no one wanted to take the blame. If no one would own up, Jesus would always be asked first and would always tell the truth. And what used to infuriate the rest of us kids was that his answers were never questioned! I know that if my word had always been accepted like that, I would have started to see what I could get away with from time to time. But it didn't work like that with Jesus.

To sum it up, I would say that he was absolutely wonderful to be with overall, but he could also be rather uncomfortable at times because he wouldn't join the rest of us in doing things that our parents wouldn't have wanted us to do.

He also had ways of providing simple explanations for things that nobody else could explain at all. I remember once he explained to the whole family what angels were and what they were like. For once, I felt that I understood.

Jesus learned how to be a carpenter and builder from Dad, and his skills were good enough to keep the family going by himself after Dad died – until I was old enough to start helping too.

He made yokes for the local farmers that never rubbed the necks of the oxen raw, and that let them pull harder than anybody else's yokes. Now he uses that idea as a teaching method, saying that his disciples should take his yoke and wear it – but he never mentions that he knows what he is talking about in crafting smooth yokes that are just right for the animals wearing them.

When people wanted Jesus to work on buildings, he used to convince them that the foundation was the most important thing. And none of the houses he has built have ever fallen down – he knows what he is talking about. He uses that picture in his preaching too, so I guess that could be why he paid so much attention to it while he was working so hard to support us as a family.

However, I'm getting off the topic and I want to get back to it. Jesus has always been rock-solid – absolutely stable, utterly dependable and willing to do anything to help anyone.

And that's what started me thinking that he might be pushing himself a bit too far and losing his mind as a result.

Thousands of people follow Jesus, but he chose just twelve of them as special disciples whom he called "apostles",[34] and he sent them out to spread the word more widely than he could do by himself. Most of them were local men, and when they came back from their tour of preaching they all met at the place where Jesus was staying.

As a family, we haven't been closely involved with everything that Jesus has been doing, but we heard recently from several different people who went to see him that the house where he was staying was constantly surrounded by crowds of people and that neither Jesus nor his apostles were ever being left alone. They weren't even being given time to eat.

Teaching, healing and helping with no time for meals or rest sounded to us like a recipe for disaster, and probably a sign of mental instability.

Our mother was particularly concerned about Jesus' health: he has always been much better at concentrating on doing God's work (as he sees it) than on looking after himself.

We shut up the workshop and we four brothers went with our mother to Capernaum. As we neared the house we could see that the reports of huge crowds were obviously true. Crowds of sick and suffering people, some with carers to help them, were clustered around every

---

[34] The Greek word translated "apostle" means an envoy, ambassador or messenger sent to carry out instructions.

door and window. Some were pushing to try to get inside, while others waited patiently. Many others in the crowd had no obvious health issues and seemed to be there just to listen, and these were always trying to quiet the noisier and more insistent members of the crowd.

Crowds filled the house[35]

It was hard to know what we should do. If we tried to get inside, we would be fighting against a crowd of people who wouldn't give up their positions easily. And if we did get to Jesus, we couldn't really say what we had to say in front of everybody anyway.

After some discussion, we decided that it would be best to send him a message asking him to come out and see us. When he came, we would then do our best to convince him to come back home with us to Nazareth so that we could nurse him back to health. Whatever happened, we needed to get him away from this crowd that just wouldn't leave him alone!

---

[35] http://freebibleimages.org/illustrations/paralysed-man-roof/ Slide 1 (Sweet Publishing/FreeBibleimages.org, CC BY-SA 3.0 Unported)

Near one of the doorways I recognised a man from Nazareth and managed to get his attention. Some of the people near us weren't happy with the noise I was making, but I managed to convey our request for Jesus to come out to meet us.

The message went in through the doorway of the house and we heard people passing it on through the rooms inside.

We waited, able to hear voices, but not to distinguish what was being said. Finally, a report came back out through the doorway and we had Jesus' answer.

He wouldn't come.

I was amazed: his mother and we, his brothers, had come specifically to visit him, and he wouldn't even come out to see us.

That seemed rude enough, but his actual words made it worse. Apparently, he said, "Who are my mother and my brothers?"

Jesus was disowning us all.

Worse than that, he was replacing us with others who he wasn't even related to. We were told that he had looked around at the people near him and said of them: "Here are my mother and my brothers! For whoever does the will of God, he is my brother and sister and mother."

I can never forget what Jesus was like as a brother as we grew up together, but his behaviour at the moment is too high-handed for me: if I don't do it his way he'll disown me! Is that a sign of madness or rudeness?

We never did get to take him home that day; in fact, we didn't even get close enough to talk to him. He refused to accept that we, his family, had any call on him at all – he considered his followers more important than us.

What should we do?

Is he mad? I know that his understanding of Scripture is second to none, but I can't accept that he is the saviour of the world or the Messiah we are all waiting for. He's my brother, not a great king! I used to play with him in the mud, and he taught me a lot of my carpentry skills – not exactly the perfect background for a religious leader, is it? How could God let the saviour of the world grow up in a poor home in Nazareth, a remote town in Galilee of the Gentiles?

No, he'll still have to do a lot more to convince me.

Sixteen

Injustice

For the true story, see Matthew 27:57-60; Mark 15:42-46; Luke 23:50-54; John 19:38-42.

Jesus of Nazareth is hanging on a cross.

I went to see the crucifixion because it felt like that was all I could do to support him in his undeserved trouble, but while I was there, I saw other members of the council. They were laughing at him and challenging him to save himself – men with whom I have sat, talked, worked and argued. I could not bear to listen to any more of what they said; it was too horrifying. So I came back here to the temple to write down my thoughts and ponder my questions.

I hate injustice.

False witnesses are an abomination to me.

Yet I have seen both of those things paraded before me during this last day, promoted as necessary and even good. I sat and listened as a man was first condemned by leaders interested solely in their own positions of power, then crucified because of the terrifying power of a ranting mob.

Jesus, the prophet from Nazareth, was arrested, tried, convicted and crucified this day for the crime of – would you believe it? – telling the truth. Our council, the Sanhedrin, so distorted God's rules that our long-awaited Messiah could not tell the truth without them convicting him of blasphemy. The only way he could have escaped alive would have been to become a liar like them.

I fought the rhetoric, I fought the decision, but I could do nothing. I did not agree that Jesus deserved any punishment, let alone death. As a member of the council, I did all I could, yet I was powerless in the face of self-centred bigots. There were only two on the council who would stand against the injustice: Nicodemus and myself. Only two who said we should reject the false witnesses and their lies. Only two against the rest; and even we two were cowed into silence as the proceedings reached their climax – and this is the peak body of Jewish justice!

False witnesses at Jesus' trial[36]

---

[36] http://freebibleimages.org/illustrations/gethsemane-peter/ Slide 14 (Sweet Publishing / FreeBibleImages, CC BY-SA 3.0 Unported)

So what did Jesus do wrong to deserve such punishment?

Well, he healed the sick; he raised the dead; he cleansed lepers; he gave sight to the blind.

Are those heinous crimes? They are not like paying blood money for betrayal; like recruiting false witnesses to convict an innocent man; like calling simple words – which the evidence shows are likely to be true – "blasphemy," simply because they are unwelcome. Yet our council has committed all of these this last day; and I am part of the council.

So what did this man do that so upset the members of the council?

He ate with sinners and taught them God's commands.

He forgave the sins of cripples and proved his credibility in doing so by healing them as well.

He worked humbly and tirelessly, receiving any who would come to hear the words of God in his mouth. If you could find Jesus at any time, day or night, he would speak to you – Nicodemus proved it when he found Jesus at night to tell him that he believed he was truly from God. Within moments, Jesus had taken him out of his depth in describing what God requires of us. That night, Israel's teacher was taught deep things by a carpenter turned prophet!

He spoke truth and wisdom as no man has ever spoken them before.

And then he practised what he preached.

These "crimes" upset many members of the council greatly because they disrupted the comfortable order of things. They threatened to make religion genuine, a matter between a man and his God where riches and power were no longer the aim. Yet even with these annoyances, he might still have been left alone had he not at the same time condemned greed, selfishness, the love of money and hypocrisy.

This teaching was the straw that broke the camel's back, and it was really for these "crimes" that he was killed. Oh that more people would commit them!

Of course, his behaviour was construed as blasphemy to win over a Jewish audience, and then as rebellion to demand action from an unwilling Roman procurator.

Necessity was all that mattered. The council decided that Jesus had to be disposed of, and any method which could work towards that goal was pre-approved. Blood money was paid to a betrayer. Lies were told and re-told. False witnesses were found – which was bad enough – and then protected from punishment when their lies did not agree – which was utterly inexcusable.

Of all of the members of the council, only Nicodemus and I opposed these actions. Yet we were too cautious, too afraid, and our words were disregarded. Our objections were passed over and spurned. Despite our repeated requests and then insistence, no record was ever made of our objections.

None of this could I stop. Yet to feel powerless against overt evil in the highest authorities in the nation is soul-destroying. Corruption in the representatives of Rome I can understand and accept. But corruption in the leaders of God's own people I can neither understand nor accept.

So now I have to make my decision: do I quit, or try to fight on? Do I fight for justice for a man who will soon be dead? Or do I join his followers even though the leader they followed can no longer lead?

Of course, it may already be too late: I may already have made too much noise and spoken too loudly against the council's decision. Maybe my position on the council is already in jeopardy. During the trial, I objected to matters of process and law, and when the question was put, I could not vote in favour of the decision to declare Jesus guilty. But I did not declare myself Jesus' disciple – although that is what I am. I was too afraid.

⌘

I couldn't keep away. I went back to Golgotha and heard a criminal, hanging on the cross next to Jesus, cursing him. Then I heard the criminal on the other side of Jesus acknowledge his own guilt and beg Jesus for forgiveness.

So then I had to return to the temple and ask myself the question: Should I do the same?

This whole episode has tested me deeply. I have been forced to think in ways I have never thought before. I grew up in a rich family in Arimathea. Comfort has been my constant companion, and our national religion fitted well into my life. The way our religion operates honours the rich and values each of them above a hundred of the poor. When I was called to take a place on the council of Israel, it seemed a fitting reward for years of responsible, community-minded living. I had a position of importance and enjoyed it.

Yet I was not heartless. I genuinely tried to keep the laws of our God as I understood them. When I sat on the council, I did try to do justly, to love mercy and to walk humbly with our God. But now I realise that my commitment to God was a limited commitment. My fellow-man's opinion of me has always been more important to me than keeping God's law. During Jesus' trial, my concern about the council's opinion kept me silent, kept me in my seat when I should have stood with Jesus. It might not have made any difference, but it would have been the right thing to do.

That thief heard the scoffing and condemnation of Jesus from his rulers and his peers, and yet still spoke out in defence of Jesus. A convicted, self-acknowledged criminal had more courage than I. I suppose he had nothing to lose. Or was he motivated by what he had to gain? Maybe what he will gain is what I will lose if I don't follow his example. Imagine that! Joseph of Arimathea, respected member of the Sanhedrin, learning a lesson from a robber, following the moral example of a robber; and all over the crucifixion of a poor carpenter.

My world is spinning out of control.

Am I brave enough to go and talk to Jesus?

Well, it is all over, and now I am waiting for Pilate's answer to my request.

When I left the temple earlier, I had decided that it was too late to do anything about Jesus. Nothing that I could do would help him anymore, and it was not worth the risk to my career to try to help a dying man anyway.

I had even decided that it was not worth returning to Golgotha just to see more hours of suffering. It was better, I thought, to put it all out of my mind, however unjust it had been.

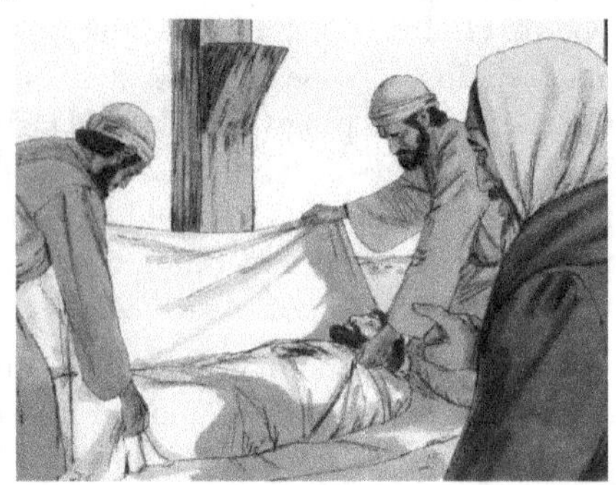

Joseph of Arimathea and Nicodemus prepare Jesus' body for burial[37]

But then, as I walked towards my house, the sun began to go strangely dark, and all of my doubts and guilt came flooding back. Immediately I changed my mind and went to Golgotha. By the time I got there, it was almost completely dark, and I waited there for hours as the darkness lingered. Some of the chief priests and other members of the council were still there, but this sudden unexplained darkness made no obvious impression on them: their laughter and abuse continued with very little letup. I stood there, near them, but not with them. Yet I could not bring myself to speak to Jesus. Some of his followers were there; I recognised them. One of them was a young man called John, who knew, and was known by,

---

[37] http://freebibleimages.org/illustrations/jesus-crucified-dies/ Slide 13 (Sweet Publishing / FreeBibleImages.org, CC BY-SA 3.0 Unported)

the High Priest – and that made me think again. He was known and recognised, yet he still stood by the cross of Jesus. His courage inspired me, but not enough; still I could not go and speak to Jesus or openly express my support for him. I kept trying to work up the courage to do so, but then, suddenly, it was all too late.

"Father, forgive them, for they know not what they do," Jesus said. His first words cut through me like a knife, for I felt strongly that I needed forgiveness, but his following words made it even worse, for I felt that I had known what I was allowing, but had let fear close my lips. Though I believed him innocent, in the end, my actions had shown that I did not consider him worth the possible loss of my consequence and reputation. I wanted the praise of men more than the praise which comes only from God.

Then Jesus shouted out with a loud voice, saying, "My God, my God, why have you forsaken me?" His voice was a bit hard to understand – his throat must have been dry after hours on the cross. Some of the people listening got mixed up about what he had said, while others went to give him a drink so that they could hear his words more clearly. In the misunderstanding, Jesus did ask for a drink, and it seemed to give him the energy for one last effort.

"It is finished," he cried, and then his head slumped forward onto his chest and that was it: Jesus was dead. I had missed my chance to speak to him.

When the centurion who was supervising the crucifixions realised that Jesus was dead, he said two things that made an impression on me, coming as they did from a heathen: "This man was innocent," he said; and then, in wonder, "This man was the son of God."

He was right in both. Suddenly I knew that he was, and also that I must do whatever I could for Jesus.

Some years ago, I had a tomb cut out of the rock in a garden near Golgotha, and it has been sitting there unused ever since. Normally, the bodies of crucified men are disposed of in the local rubbish dump, where they are burned to ash with the other rubbish of society, and I knew that that was where Jesus' body would go if I continued to keep quiet. Suddenly I found the courage and determination to stand up against the chief priests and their ilk. I would go and ask for the body of Jesus and bury it in my tomb. What better way was left to me to declare my support for him and for the kingdom of God which he had preached? Immediately, I went directly to Pilate and asked for the body of Jesus. It was a situation in which I was able to use my position for good; he would never have even considered the request if it had come from any of Jesus' known followers.

So now I am waiting for his answer. Waiting while he checks that Jesus is really dead.

CR

The day is over and the Passover has begun. It is a special Sabbath today, yet I am unclean through contact with a dead body – the body of Jesus. This month, I cannot eat of the Passover in memory of God's deliverance of my people from Egypt.

But although I am sorry to miss the Passover, I think it was worth it, and Nicodemus agrees.

As I waited for Pilate's answer, I thought carefully about what to do, and decided to ask Nicodemus to come and help me. It was a big thing to ask of him, since he too is on the council, and likewise stood to lose his position in society if he showed support for Jesus. He agreed immediately, though, and even offered to bring the mixture of myrrh and aloes that we use for a burial. I think he feels as guilty as I do.

Once Pilate gave me permission to take the body, I took the linen shroud I had bought and went with Nicodemus to arrange the burial. Together we took down the body, with the help of the centurion and his men.

Apparently, the High Priest had heard about our plans to bury Jesus, because he sent some of his servants to watch what we did. It must have been a big surprise to them to hear that Jesus' body would not be burned as they had expected – and probably wanted. I'm glad that we upset that much of their plans. I just wish we had been able to stop their plans to kill Jesus in the first place.

Human bodies are heavy, but both Nicodemus and I were amazed at how light Jesus' body was. He could multiply loaves and fish enough to feed thousands, but he clearly didn't feed himself that way! People had welcomed him into their homes and provided great feasts for him, but it was obvious that he had concentrated on the people who were there rather than on the food itself. His body was like that of an old man who is worn out with hard work. Now, anyone who took any interest at all in Jesus knew that he took no comforts for himself, but preparing his gaunt body for burial highlighted this to me so very clearly.

Nicodemus and I carried the body very carefully to my tomb on a stretcher. Nicodemus' servant carried the spices and my servant carried the linen cloths and the shroud. We could have had our servants carry the body, but that didn't seem quite right. We were the ones who wanted to make sure he was buried. We were the ones who felt the guilt, and were willing to make ourselves unclean to make amends as best we could.

∝

There is a certain irony in the idea that the chief priests and members of the council who lied and cheated to kill an innocent man can eat the Passover feast, confident that they are clean, while Nicodemus and I must not eat because we did what we could to give the son of God the honourable burial he deserved.

None of Jesus' day-to-day followers could ever have got permission from Pilate, and even if they had miraculously done so, the chief priests would have been sure to have followed with the temple guard and taken the body away to dispose of it. And where would Jesus' followers have buried their Lord anyway? My position on the council, and Nicodemus' as well, gave Jesus the burial he deserved.

Whatever this may cost us, the cost is worthwhile. Jesus was the son of God.

Seventeen

All, or Not Quite?

For the true story, see Acts 4:32-5:11.

First 120, then another 3,000 in one day, then climbing to 5,000, the number of believers in Jesus kept rising astronomically. Despite the beatings and imprisonment of the leaders, people continued to find the teachings of Jesus and the infectious fellowship of his followers irresistible. There was a feeling of astonishing excitement and newness after the self-centred and stale religion of the scribes and Pharisees. As for the Sadducees, their religion was even worse, focusing as it did on political power and money.

No, the believers had something wonderful to offer that the established religions could not compete with, and the feeling of possible danger didn't put most people off at all.

But it wasn't long before the initial enthusiasm began to pall a little. Religious zeal is all very well for religious zealots, but most people are too practical for that. There was this idea of sharing everything amongst the believers, and so various people had the opportunity to get noticed by giving some of their goods for everybody to use. The givers were noticed and praised, and everyone was happy.

One of the eager enthusiasts, however, a Levite named Joseph who had been born in Cyprus, raised the bar. He wasn't satisfied with just a medium-value gift: instead, he sold a field he owned and gave the money – all of it – to the apostles for distribution.

That certainly made it more difficult to get noticed amongst "the believers", as they called themselves.

But one couple, Ananias and Sapphira, came up with an ingenious plan to give and to get noticed, while keeping a little nest-egg just in case.

It really was ingenious.

Let me tell you about it.

Stage 1

They had a piece of property that would be worth quite a bit of money if they sold it. Then they could give some of the proceeds to the apostles and everyone would take note that they, Ananias and Sapphira, had given so very generously. Good will and a measure of fame would come to them because everyone would hear of their outstanding generosity.

So they sold the property, and got a good price, too – but they didn't tell anyone else. Not yet.

They wanted to help the poor, no question about that, but... if they gave away all the money, what would happen if they needed some? How would they be able to afford those small indulgences that made life a little more joyful? Keeping some of the money was obviously the best thing to do.

Stage 2

As the day for settling the deal drew nearer, one or other of the pair had a marvellous idea, a once-in-a-lifetime piece of brilliance: keep some of the money, but tell the apostles that they had given all of it!

Yes, they both agreed, that was the best thing to do.

After all, helping the poor was important to them. Just think of those fatherless children they had heard of last week, and the widows whose children had rejected them when they joined the believers.

They certainly saw themselves as people who helped the poor and gave to those less fortunate than themselves.

As for the slight tampering with the truth, that was nothing major. Without doubt, the amount they were giving was the important detail. No-one would ever know.

Stage 3

The money was in their hands and it felt good. The money they were keeping for themselves had been separated from the rest of the money already.

What an opportunity to use the remainder to help all of their brothers and sisters in the faith! So much being given to help so many, with just a part being kept for themselves – only a small part, really.

Everybody would be so glad to see the love of Ananias and Sapphira being shown in genuine action, and doubtless others would be encouraged to follow and continue the outworking of faith.

It was time to hand over the money to the apostles:

Ananias would deliver it. They both hoped that there would be enough witnesses that their generosity would be reported widely among the believers without them needing to assist.

A few witnesses would be a very good thing.

Stage 4

Ananias carried the money in a bag to the room where the apostles could normally be found when they were not out preaching. Entering the room, he had to wait a few minutes while the apostles dealt with another matter.

Looking around, he was pleased to see that there were quite a few witnesses, including some young men who would be sure to treat him with much more respect after this.

He spent the time reflecting on just how clever their plan was and the admiration and respect they would soon be receiving.

Soon, Ananias was called forward and asked what his business was.

"I and Sapphira my wife sold a piece of property," announced Ananias, "and we have decided to give all of the proceeds to help any believers who are needy."

There were a few rather pleasing gasps around the room, and several people turned to look at each other, exchanging glances of shared admiration for such generosity.

But Peter wasn't looking so pleased as he stood up and walked across to Ananias. Ananias looked into his eyes and saw condemnation there. He wondered briefly whether Peter could have heard of their plans, but he knew there was no way that Peter could know their clever ruse, so he waited to hear what the great apostle had to say.

"Ananias," said Peter, "why has Satan filled your heart to lie to the Holy Spirit and to keep back for yourself part of the proceeds of the land? While it remained unsold, did it not remain your own? And after it was sold, was it not at your disposal? Why is it that you have contrived this deed in your heart? You have not lied to man but to God."

The dreams and plans were suddenly torn away as Ananias fell down like a stone, dead. Instead of witnessing his triumph, those present witnessed his downfall. Those young men watching did not learn to show him respect; rather, they wound him up in grave clothes and took him out and buried him.

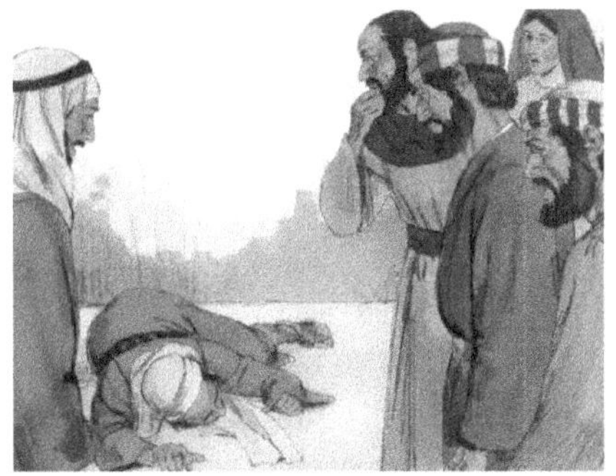

When Ananias heard what Peter said, he fell down dead[38]

Stage 5

It was about three hours later when Sapphira came to the apostles, looking for her husband, and perhaps looking for some praise for their generosity.

She entered a room made serious by the unexpected death of her husband. Sensing that something important or serious had taken place, she felt the gravity of the situation, but suspected nothing.

The apostle Peter had a difficult task to complete. Nothing like this had ever happened in their fellowship before, and the horror of it was still sinking in. Hiding the truth from God was impossible, of course, and that was how Peter had known of Ananias' crime. Lying to God was a very serious crime, and God had judged it worthy of death.

Peter wondered whether Sapphira would admit their plot, acknowledge their guilt. Maybe God would spare her if she did. The matter must be settled immediately.

"Tell me," he asked, solemnly, "whether you sold the land for so much."

Briefly, she wondered whether Ananias had somehow given away the secret – but no, he knew just how important it was. There was no way he would let it out. No-one could possibly know.

"Yes," she said, "for so much."

Peter said to her, "How is it that you have agreed together to test the Spirit of the Lord? Behold, the feet of those who have buried your husband are at the door, and they will carry you out."

Sapphira's dreams of being shown respect and admiration died with her, as she likewise fell to the floor before Peter.

Only a short time later, the young men who had carried the body of Ananias to its burial came in and found his wife dead too.

"What happened?" asked their leader.

"They had agreed together to lie to God," explained Peter. "Sapphira confirmed that they had sold the land for the amount of money that they gave, and yet the Holy Spirit revealed to me that they had kept some for themselves. God has killed them both."

"So was it that they didn't give all of the money?" asked one of the young men.

"No," replied Peter, "it was the lie they told. If they had come to us and said, 'Here is some of the money we made from the sale of our property,' they would both still be alive. Their lies led to death. Never forget that God is a God of truth."

Stage 6

Attempting to earn respect through deceit didn't work. Ananias and his wife Sapphira paid the ultimate price for their lies, and all the believers heard the terrible tale. Those who had viewed this new religion as an exciting new opportunity to dabble in religion found that suddenly they had to take it seriously. Very seriously.

All of the believers, every last one of them, realised once again that God sees and knows. Nothing can be hidden from him.

Have you learned that lesson yet?

Eighteen

Cornelius

For the true story, see Acts 10:1-48.

Ten cohorts make up a Roman legion, and with 30 legions, Rome maintains peace in the habitable world. The so-called "Italian Cohort" is headquartered in Caesarea, and its 400 men form five centuries, each with a centurion in command.

Cornelius is one of these centurions, one of maybe 3,000 across the empire – but no ordinary centurion is Cornelius.

He wouldn't want me to write this about him, but he is a devout man who fears God and inspires his entire household to do the same. Not only that, but he is generous with his income, giving to any who have need.

Does that sound like an ordinary centurion to you?

Of course not, but that's not all. The Roman army is built on discipline and all centurions depend on it. However, Cornelius also applies discipline to himself: he prays continually.

Well, all of these outstanding qualities must have pleased God too, because one afternoon while Cornelius was praying, God sent an angel to give him some instructions.

Being who he is, Cornelius decided that if these instructions were important enough for God to send him an angel, they must be urgent, so he immediately called two of his personal servants and a soldier who was also a worshipper of God. He quickly passed on the instructions and told them to leave first thing in the morning. The journey would take about a day and a half,[39] so there was no advantage in trying to leave that night. If they left at daybreak, they could travel all day and arrive sometime around noon on the following day.

As any experienced centurion would, Cornelius carefully calculated how long various components of the journey would take and discussed the results with the messengers he was sending. Tomorrow they would stop for the night about two thirds of the way to Joppa. The following day would take them to Joppa and give them time to find the man they were looking for and arrange for him to return with them.

"But what if he won't come?" asked the soldier.

"Don't worry, he will come – God will make sure that he is ready and willing. Then, if you set off again the next morning, you should arrive back here with him at about mid-afternoon on the fourth day."

"Yes, sir, we'll do our best."

Cornelius smiled at the three men and said, "Don't worry, it will work."

---

[39] From Caesarea to Joppa is 60km (37 miles).

Four days later, they were back and Cornelius was waiting for them, with his relatives and close friends in attendance. There, I told you that he isn't an ordinary centurion, and you can tell for yourself that he isn't an ordinary man either; he has *extraordinary* faith.

As far as could be told, he was not even mildly impressed that, when his messengers had arrived in Joppa and asked for the house of Simon the tanner, they had been shown immediately to a house beside the sea – exactly as the angel had said. His family and friends were all intrigued to hear how the three had arrived at the house and called out to ask if a man called Simon was staying there, only to be met by the man himself as he came down the stairs from the roof! But Cornelius seemed simply to expect it.

Then, when he was introduced to Simon Peter, he revealed another of his amazing characteristics: humility. He, a Roman centurion, bowed down to this unknown Jew – who turned out to be merely an uneducated Galilean fisherman! Well, Peter immediately lifted him up again, saying that he was a man just the same as Cornelius and should not be worshipped.

It was only when Peter explained about a vision that God had shown him while he was up on the roof that Cornelius began to marvel at the extent of God's preparation for this event. Peter described his vision of a great sheet being let down from heaven, full of all sorts of unclean animals, and the instruction that he should kill and eat. He also told how, when he had expressed his disgust at the idea, a voice had insisted three times that what God had made clean, he, Peter, should not call common.

Peter saw heaven opened and a sheet coming down, full of unclean animals, reptiles and birds[40]

Cornelius could see that the vision had been given at just the right time to achieve what God wanted. He was amazed that God should have performed such a marvel for him, his family and friends. This demonstration of God's planning going so far beyond what he had expected delighted Cornelius.

It was wonderful to watch as the fisherman spoke to the centurion. An experienced centurion like Cornelius is used to being the one in authority while others obey, yet his attitude toward Peter was that of a man who needed help and was willing to beg for it. Peter, in his turn, displayed none of the grudging acknowledgement of the Roman soldier that is typical of the conquered peoples of the empire. Instead, he showed genuine pleasure in knowing that someone wanted to hear about the God of Israel, and about Jesus, his master and closest friend.

---

[40] http://freebibleimages.org/illustrations/peter-cornelius/ Slide 7 (Sweet Publishing / FreeBibleImages.org, CC BY-SA 3.0 Unported)

It was clear from the start that there was a meeting of minds as two righteous men conferred, eager to come to understand God better together. As a Jew, Peter had the advantage of a background in God's laws, but now he was seeing an opportunity opening up for the Gentiles that he didn't quite understand. On the other hand, Cornelius was beginning to sense that God was actually inviting him to join a fellowship in which he could genuinely take a part, rather than being only an observer.

Simon Peter and his six companions were enthralled by Cornelius' explanation of God's unexpected intervention in his life. Peter marvelled at this foreigner's willingness to risk losing the respect of his family and friends, his standing in society, and even his job itself. Of course, he already knew from Cornelius' messengers that their master was dedicated to the Jewish religion, seeing in its laws a beauty and justice that he could not resist, but this was going even further. And Peter was also astonished at God's obvious approval of this Gentile's attitude, to the extent that an angel had been dispatched to instruct him how to find the truth about Jesus that leads to salvation.

Nobody quite knew where this meeting would – or should – lead. God had arranged it, so the people involved were trying to feel their way within the framework that God had established. Peter knew that God had pronounced these people clean, so he must enter these unfamiliar surroundings amid such unfamiliar company, and be ready to speak to them about Jesus. Cornelius knew that he was about to hear something from Peter that God considered important enough to warrant sending him an angel from heaven.

The excitement in the room was almost palpable as Cornelius invited Peter to tell everyone all that he had been commanded to speak.

So Peter spoke and told them all about the good news of peace that had come through Jesus. He reminded them of the events that they all knew about: how Jesus had been baptised by John the Baptist and anointed by the Holy Spirit. Speaking with the conviction of a true eyewitness, Peter recounted how Jesus had travelled about doing good and healing many. His eyes shone as he described the master he had walked with; even the painful story of Jesus' death could not take away the joy in his voice because of the glorious resurrection that had surprised them all just three days later.

Cornelius and the rest of the audience had heard the rumours of resurrection, but now they were hearing of it from a man who had actually eaten and drunk with Jesus after his resurrection. Cornelius didn't mention it, but he had also heard from many sneering Roman soldiers about how Jesus had been completely abandoned by his followers even before he was killed. He knew that Peter had been one of the followers who had abandoned Jesus, which made his infectious certainty about Jesus' resurrection all the more compelling. Despite having been too afraid to stand beside his leader at his trial and execution, Peter was now willing to stand up for Jesus because he was certain that he was alive. Cornelius found it utterly convincing.

Peter went on to report how Jesus had commanded his followers to preach the hope of salvation and the forgiveness of sins – and how thousands of Jews had already answered the call.

As Cornelius listened, he felt a growing closeness to

God and an inexpressible thankfulness for God's generosity in sending Jesus – and in sending the angel as well. Then, suddenly, it was as if the power of God was inside him: the closeness was greater than he had ever believed possible. All at once, the rumours he had heard about how these followers of Jesus were able to speak in foreign languages were confirmed. Aramaic, that difficult language that the Jews spoke among themselves, was inside his mind, coming out of his mouth in words of complete understanding. He praised God in Aramaic and saw Peter stare at him in astonishment. His family, his friends, his devout soldiers, all were speaking to each other in many different languages, but mostly, they seemed to be speaking to God, praising him and giving him glory.

Broad smiles lit up the faces of all the Gentiles who had received this incredible gift of the Holy Spirit, and Cornelius almost laughed at the amazement on the faces of Peter and the believers who had come with him. Clearly they had not expected anything like this!

It was God's work; God's miracle; God's clear lesson. Nobody could possibly deny God's decision to include the Gentiles in his chosen flock.

Cornelius and all who had responded to his invitation to listen to Peter were baptised in the name of the Lord Jesus, and as Cornelius gazed around at everyone afterwards with a look of wonder in his eyes and a smile of joy on his lips, he kept shaking his head. God's preparation and liberality had left even him speechless.

God truly had heard Cornelius' prayers and seen his generosity. And since then, millions of Gentiles have benefited from his prayer that fateful afternoon in Caesarea: Gentiles too can become children of Abraham.

Nineteen

A Touch of Magic

For the true story, see Acts 13:6-12.

Well, I have to admit, I really don't know how he did it. He is clearly a better showman than I am! But I'll get back to that later.

My father taught me all that I know about magic and being a magician. Of course, the two things are quite different, as you would understand.

Magic is using supernatural forces to do impossible things. You must know, as I do, that this is impossible. Supernatural forces are only good for superstitious people.

Being a magician is appearing to use supernatural forces to do impossible things, and that is truly an art. More than that, it is my calling, my vocation – and normally my triumph.

From right when I was very young, my father saw in me the perfect pupil. He told me that I was learning from the best magician there was, and that if even half of his skill could rub off on me, I would be without equal – once he was dead.

So he said.

The fact was, however, that, although my father would never admit it, I had surpassed him in skill before ever I reached my 15th birthday. Not only that, but my gift of showmanship allowed me to present my unequalled skill in a way that may never have been seen before in the history of the world.

Quite simply, no-one can believe that the things I do as a magician are anything but genuine. They all believe that I am genuinely performing magic.

But sleight of hand is natural for me. I can transfer an egg from my hand to my sleeve so that nobody – and I mean nobody – could ever see me do it. Hours of practice, and my father's stick of encouragement, honed my skills so perfectly that I can perform any of these tricks with one hand, even while performing acrobatics and running smoothly through my patter. These are my abilities, but I rarely use even half of them. I have found it much better to take a step back from trying to discover whether I have any limitations in this field. Like many magicians before me, I have also found that adding a religious flavour to my performance gains me much more long-lasting fame and – more importantly – a much greater income and influence. Long flowing robes, darkness, incense, and a deep, mysterious voice all help to sway an audience. I am still young, but I have no doubt that I am destined for greatness in Rome, the centre of both the empire and religion – once I get over my current difficulties.

Already, thousands of people admire me for my magic and many treat me as a religious phenomenon. Of course, I know it's all fake, but I make the most of the well-earned adulation.

Cyprus is a bit of a cultural backwater, but it has been a good place to learn the tricks of wielding influence. The proconsul Sergius Paulus is an intelligent man and has real integrity, so I have been using my skills to manipulate him. It can be quite challenging at times, but a light and careful touch can still bamboozle even a clever man. Over the last year, I have been gradually worming my way into his confidence, never making it too obvious, but making the most of every opportunity.

Yes, everything was going fine until these troublemakers, Paul and Barnabas, turned up. At first, I thought they were just religious cranks, but then I heard some reports of miracles they had performed, and realised that I had some truly expert magicians to compete with.

Candle[41]

Get this – they were performing "healings" outdoors in broad daylight. No quiet rooms, helpful assistants, waving lamps, offerings to the gods, or incense. Nothing. When I heard that, I knew these really were magicians worthy of my mettle.

---

[41] https://openclipart.org/detail/117187/candle by Andy_Gardiner (OpenClipArt)

Naturally, I had confidence that I could outperform them, but I very quickly found that I would have to make a move forthwith. You see, Sergius Paulus heard about them and their teachings and called them in for an interview.

Since I had the proconsul's ear, it wasn't hard to make sure that I was present at the interview. Paul was the leader, despite being the smaller of the two. Very intense he was, too – none of the aloofness in presentation that I have found so effective. I must say he uses the strategy very well, though, giving a convincing impression that he passionately believes the things he is speaking about.

I was very impressed by his technique.

He was speaking to Sergius Paulus about the Jewish religion, but added a new twist about a man called Jesus, whom Paul claimed had been raised from the dead. Now I know all about the Jewish religion – after all, I am a Jew myself – and weave many of our religious themes into my own words, but I am always very careful to respectfully acknowledge the Roman religion. Success in the highest circles of the empire will only be possible if I follow this path, blending the ancient and modern, acknowledging all of Rome's pantheon while bringing in the wisdom and proverbs of the Jewish scriptures. I know it sounds like a difficult mix, but I have the skill for it.

But Paul was intriguing. He was able to sound completely convincing. No-one who listened to him could doubt for a moment that he believed every word he spoke. Well, no-one except me, that is, but that's because I'm a professional too, so I can see through all that stuff.

Very quickly I could see that I needed to somehow do something to stop him, and soon, or else all my influence with Sergius Paulus would be lost. Paul's skill in presenting religious arguments as if they were logical was quite disconcerting, and as the proconsul listened, I could see that he was being drawn in by all that claptrap.

So I started to drop in a few spoilers. Snide remarks, sarcastic questions, clever asides – anything I could think of to raise doubts and damage Paul's credibility.

Maybe I lacked my usual deft smoothness, but if I did, it was due only to my growing concern that this time I had an opponent who might not be so easy to defeat.

All of a sudden, Paul turned and looked straight at me – and I have never seen such power in a man's eyes!

"You son of the devil," he said to me, and then he went on to say all sorts of things about me that I don't care to repeat.

The accusation he seemed to consider the most important was that I was making crooked the straight paths of the Lord. Well, really! Everyone who dabbles in religion is doing that, aren't they? All great preachers are just trying to point people in the direction that suits them, the way that transfers the largest quantities of gold from the pockets of the faithful to the pockets of the preacher! Did this Paul really have the gall to suggest that he was any different?

But then came the most stunning part of his performance, the part that I am still trying to understand.

He didn't even build up to it with a theatrical wave of the arms or anything like that. With no real change in pitch – I could have presented it much better, I'm sure – he simply said, "Behold, the hand of the Lord is upon you, and you will be blind and unable to see the sun for a time."

Immediately it was as if I was looking through mist, and within a few terrifying moments, complete darkness had spread across my vision.

For days, whenever I wanted to go anywhere I was forced to find people to lead me by the hand.

And ever since, I have been trying to work out how he did it. What was his trick? As a professional, I'm suitably impressed by his methods, and I have to find out how it works. I've concluded that it must have been something that he threw into my eyes, but I didn't see it coming, or feel it either. That incredibly intent look must have been part of the trick. He must have used it to hold my attention so completely that I didn't notice the powder coming – or whatever it was.

I tried cleaning it off. First I tried using water, but without success. I couldn't even feel anything in my eyes, so if it was a powder it must have been incredibly fine.

After that, I tried putting some salt in the water, but it made no difference. Next I tried using milk, but that didn't work either. By then I suppose that my servant must have been getting tired of my demands, because he made the foolish suggestion that maybe it really was the power of God! I suppose that slaves are all superstitious and can't understand that the gods don't really exist, but are merely figments of superstitious imaginations that are used by people like me and Paul to wield power over the ignorant masses.

Clearly, and I hate to admit this, Paul has a greater skill than I in this arena.

I had to keep trying to find out what he had done.

Next I tried using soap, and that felt like I was burning my eyes out but had no other effect. The blackness stayed just as black.

Wine, vinegar, even lemon juice made no difference, except that my eyes were gradually getting more and more sore.

After a few days, I was close to giving up. I was still very impressed by Paul's skill, but not so pleased with being blind.

Then suddenly I noticed that, for the first time since it had happened, I could actually see a little light. Slowly, it got better until finally I could see properly again – just as Paul had said.

Now how did he do that? It was the final, crowning touch that would completely convince his audience that he could foretell the future.

I am lost in complete and utter admiration. I cannot find any higher praise for Paul than to say that he is a true Magician. His performance was absolutely masterful, from beginning to end. If only he and I could get together in the business, we could take Rome by storm. I could show him how to work the audience a bit better, and he could show me the potions or powders he uses. But maybe he'd reckon that he doesn't need me.

I'll have to try to talk to him again, maybe once my eyes start to feel a bit better.

Twenty

I Must Have Gone to Sleep

For the true story, see Acts 20:7-12.

Most people don't get teased for dying, but I do.

When we meet together to worship God, if I ever go and sit near the window, someone in the congregation is sure to say, "Oh, no you don't! We all know what happens when you sit there!"

If a meeting is being arranged at a house we haven't been to before, someone always has to ask the householder, "Do all of the windows have bars across them?" And then they both look across at me, slyly.

It's not a great feeling to be the one who everyone remembers as the man who went to sleep while brother Paul was talking.

I suppose the strangest thing about the whole episode is that I don't actually remember any of the important parts, the parts that everyone laughs about.

It was at the very start of spring that Tychicus and Trophimus arrived in Troas and reported that Paul and several of his other friends and helpers would be visiting soon. Naturally, we were very excited, looking forward to seeing them again, and hearing more news and encouragement.

Tychicus and Trophimus also told us about the time Paul had spent in Macedonia and Greece after that amazing riot in Ephesus, a riot that sort of fizzled into apathy after the town clerk gave the crowd a stern warning. Don't think that Paul's enemies left him alone, though. Apparently, just as he was about to set sail from Greece, the Jews again made plans to kill him. I can't help wondering whether sometime they might succeed, but obviously Jesus still has work for Paul to do in his name – Paul keeps escaping. He is just so brave, too. I don't think that I would have been so very eager to go back into Macedonia if I were Paul. The Jews of the area have tried to kill him several times in several places. But he has complete confidence that they will continue to fail until his work is finished.

It was less than two weeks after Passover when they all arrived, having come by ship from Macedonia. Passover is still an important time to many of the Jewish believers, and to us Gentiles as well. After all, Jesus died and was raised at this time of year about 25 years ago, and Peter was freed from prison on the last day of the Feast of Unleavened Bread about 13 or so years ago. Not only that, but John's beloved brother James was killed a little before that same feast, so these are times when we have much to remember. Of course, I am too young to remember any of those actual events – I wasn't even born when Jesus ascended into heaven. But I love to hear the stories from the people who do remember them, and Paul can tell some amazing tales of his own life, too.

We had a whole week – seven wonderful days – of listening to his teaching and his stories, hanging on his every word as he explained details about history and the Jewish law that I had never even thought about. It is amazing how much more everything means when you know more about the background. I'm not a Jew, but I often catch myself thinking of Abraham as my natural ancestor because I get so used to thinking about his family tree and the way he lived. It has all become more a part of me than my own family tree with its ingrained idolatry – and those other tawdry details that no-one in the family ever wants to talk about.

Every evening, we all gathered together and listened to Paul and the other visitors talking about God's work around the world, and his work through righteous people in many different times. Back then, nobody ever introduced the speakers with words like, "Tonight, the brother with the job of keeping Eutychus awake is…" Now they often do. I try to be patient.

But how those brothers made the word of God come to life! One evening, Noah's faith was made so real that the next morning I couldn't help imagining myself getting up for another day of ship building, building that enormous monument to faith that saved life on God's earth. And when it started to rain on me the next afternoon, I imagined the ark slowly starting to float with its precious cargo. At the time, I was placing a wooden beam to support the new roof on an extra floor that my master is building for a customer, but that didn't stop my imagination seeing the ark standing rugged and safe as the sudden disaster engulfed those around. What a magnificent testament to a strong and steady faith. Ah, the encouragement that others can give us through their faith!

Then, sadly, the seven days were coming to an end and the first day of the week came. As usual, we met together to break bread, and Paul spoke to us.

I really enjoy listening to Paul speaking, but his style is a bit unusual. He can be talking about a subject in fine detail and be just about to examine some small point when suddenly he jumps to a completely different subject, and never quite gets back to the first point. Some of the brothers find it distracting and end up feeling a bit cheated, but I find that he gives me lots to think about from what he does say, while also leaving me with many things to think about that he didn't get around to saying!

But on that last evening it was quite warm, and the room was pretty full. The older ones sat closer to Paul so that they could hear him, while we younger ones sat against the walls around the edges. I was sitting on the window sill where the frame was set into the thick walls of the upper room in which we were meeting.

The way people tell it now, you would think that I went to sleep as soon as Paul started speaking, but it wasn't that way at all. In fact, I saw lots of others snoozing much earlier in the evening while Paul talked on and on. It didn't hurt anyone. People listened while they were awake, then snoozed for a while before awaking again ready to listen some more.

And there was plenty more to listen to!

Paul spoke on for three hours, four hours, five hours, and by then I was starting to have a problem. It was quite stuffy in the room, and every so often I leaned out of the window a bit to get some fresh air, to help me stay awake. But it was getting harder and harder. Some of the sentences I heard weren't making any sense at all – I suppose I was missing bits in the middle – but I kept struggling on.

Eutychus fell into a deep sleep and then fell out of the window[42]

And that's all I remember – until suddenly I saw Paul bending over me, with others crowding around holding up lights. He had a smile on his face and he was telling everyone not to worry because I would be alright. I tried to work out what was going on – it was just like waking up from a deep sleep – and slowly realised that Paul had his arms around me too. He kept looking at me as if demanding that I wake up. Now Paul is not a man who is easy to resist, so I did my best, and after a while, I was able to sit up. That was when the big surprise really hit me, because we were outside on the street, and I had been lying on the cobblestones. Sleep sometimes leaves me

---

[42] http://freebibleimages.org/illustrations/paul-troas-miletus/ Slide 11 (Sweet Publishing / FreeBibleImages.org, CC BY-SA 3.0 Unported)

feeling a bit disoriented, but that couldn't explain how things were then.

It was only later that people explained to me that I must have gone to sleep and fallen out of the window, causing sudden consternation amongst the entire audience, and Paul in particular. I imagine it would be horrible to feel that you were the preacher who had put someone to sleep so that they fell to their death! And that's what everyone tells me happened. They say that when people got down to the street and found me, there was no doubt that I was dead. What a way to die!

Apparently, though, Paul had also hurried down and quickly reassured them that I would be alright, and so I was. After I woke up, we went back upstairs, and finally got to breaking bread together. We asked Paul to keep talking, too – after all, the ruckus had woken everyone up very thoroughly! At daybreak, he and his companions had to leave, while most of us had to go to work. It was a hard day, that one, but Paul had given us a lot to think about, so that helped to keep some of us awake. Me at least.

I don't know how much you have ever thought about the miracles of Jesus, Peter, John, Paul and others, but when God does miracles, they are done properly. I didn't even have a headache. No broken bones, nor even any bruising. All I had to remind me of what had happened was the dirt from the street on my clothes. It was really ground-in dirt, too, exactly the sort of stains that would remind me just how hard I must have hit the ground.

I have been given another chance. More days to become more like Paul. He was my hero before, but now

I feel even more attached to him. Without him and the power of God, I wouldn't be alive at all.

So now in our congregation, if anyone is feeling tired and is suddenly brought abruptly back to wakefulness after the shortest of snoozes, everyone calls it a "Eutychus moment".

In fact, if I stay awake when someone speaks to the congregation – as I almost always do – people praise me for staying awake. It's completely unfair, but I suppose people enjoy it, and it really won't hurt me too much. It just hurts my pride.

No doubt people will still be talking about me and my embarrassing gaffe hundreds of years from now!

Twenty-One

Travels with Paul

For the true story, see Acts 16:1-18:18; 19:22-20:38 as well as the two letters Paul wrote to Timothy.

My father never had any patience with what he called "Jewish myths". Yet he had chosen to marry a Jewish wife, and, paradoxically, appreciated my mother's faithfulness and the godliness[43] that came from her belief in those same so-called "myths".

He always liked clever arguments that used words as finely crafted weapons, deftly directed to lampoon an opponent's arguments and hold him up to ridicule. Debating was in his blood and the verbal cut and thrust of argument delighted him. In fact, he cared more about how an argument was presented than whether or not it was right.

In contrast, my mother was only concerned with truth. Be it ever so well presented, no argument carried any weight with her unless it bore the stamp of truth.

---

[43] 2 Timothy 1:5

From time to time, my father used to ridicule what he called her "preoccupation with truth". Yet he was proud of it too. He was very pleased that he could rely on her to always tell the truth, and insisted that I be the same.

However, my father was harsh with me at times because he wanted me to have respect for the Greek gods and to strive for glory as the demi-gods constantly did. But to me the gods deserved no respect, if any of the tales told about them were true. And the heroes like Hercules, Odysseus and Achilles didn't impress me either – they seemed to be much the same as the gods they acknowledged. The heroes of my mother's and grandmother's[44] stories from Jewish history earned my respect far more, and they never demanded, or even wanted, my worship.

Abraham, Isaac and Jacob were not perfect, but they were admirable. The heroes of the Bible were presented as men of faith whose amazing deeds came from their faith, not from pride or self-confidence.

"You just like that sort of hero because you don't have any physical courage yourself," my father said to me once. There may have been some truth in what he said – I was always a quiet and retiring child, although I was not afraid of hard work. But putting myself forward as a brave hero was not my natural bent.

Whatever the reason, I did admire quiet heroes, particularly the ones in the Hebrew Scriptures, of whom I had heard from my childhood. I knew that there was only one God and that the gods presented by other nations were frauds. One God, the creator of everything else,

---

[44] 2 Timothy 1:5

made sense to me, and humble heroes attracted me much more than loud-mouthed, opinionated, self-seeking heroes who knew of nothing but self-aggrandisement.

As I grew up, my father and I quarrelled often, and sometimes the arguments spread to include my mother, which made her life difficult.

Having been learning about the Hebrew scriptures from my earliest remembrance,[45] I was a committed follower of the God of the Hebrews – I suppose you might describe me as one who feared God but was not a complete convert, in that I had not been circumcised.

I was still quite young when I heard about Jesus, the one whom some claimed was the promised Messiah. After examining the facts, I found them convincing and was baptised in the name of Jesus.

Not long afterwards, I met Paul, the apostle of Jesus Christ, and everything came to a head. My father said that if I wanted to become one of those *Christians* – of course, he used the name as a term of contempt – then I wasn't welcome in his house. Naturally, he knew that my mother, his wife, was also a Christian, but neither of us mentioned that. I didn't want to cause her any more trouble.

Both then and over the years until my father died, she kept doing her silent best to show that following the Christ was the best way to live. But I had to find somewhere else to live.

---

[45] 2 Timothy 3:15

At Lystra, Paul met a young believer named Timothy[46]

Paul was kind enough to offer to take me with him as he travelled, but there was one requirement. Since Paul's method of preaching was always to start in each new town by going to the synagogue, and the Jews all know that my father is a Greek, Paul thought that it would be best to circumcise me or I wouldn't be able to be involved in most of his preaching. In the end, it actually became a bit of a problem for me because people used me as proof that Gentiles should be circumcised (which was a pity, as it is exactly the opposite of what Paul believed), but at the time, it meant that I could travel with Paul, and that was a magnificent opportunity. It was like travelling with my own personal hero. I had been born too late to travel with Jesus as his disciple, but I could travel with Paul, and that made serving God so much easier. Paul was brave, Paul was wise, Paul was courageous, Paul always knew the right words to use, Paul was, well, Paul! – and I have never known anyone like him. I have tried desperately to imitate

---

[46] http://freebibleimages.org/illustrations/paul-antioch-philippi/ Slide 7 (Sweet Publishing / FreeBibleImages.org CC BY-SA 3.0 Unported)

him, but I don't feel that I do a very good job, particularly when it comes to handling conflict or opposition.

I have been very blessed in my life since I was forced to leave home. I travelled with Paul for the rest of his second preaching tour until he left me in Corinth and Macedonia when he returned to Antioch. After he began his third preaching tour, he sent for Erastus and me to come to him in Ephesus.[47] After working with him there for a while, he sent me back to Corinth to see how they had responded to his letter,[48] and I was so pleased that he considered me a reliable messenger. When I arrived, I found that the believers in Corinth had been very much upset by Paul's letter, and it wasn't long before I returned to him with a mixture of good and bad news.

Immediately, Paul invited me to help him write a letter to the believers at Corinth to answer some of their questions and problems.[49]

Paul then sent Erastus and me into Macedonia while he stayed in Ephesus and endured a terrifying riot there. I wasn't sorry to miss that little bit of excitement! Afterwards, he came and joined us in Macedonia and we travelled with him through Macedonia and Greece. While we were there in Corinth, Paul wrote to the believers in Rome.[50]

I mention these things because they show the way in which Paul worked and the lessons he taught me. Unfortunately, I have never felt able to do the work as well

---

[47] Acts 19:21-22

[48] 1 Corinthians 16:10

[49] 2 Corinthians 1:1

[50] Romans 16:21

as he did. Most concerning to me were his predictions that some believers would attack the flock like wolves – words that, sadly, have been proved right many times since then.

Paul was indefatigable, a tireless worker, but Jesus' plans took him away from direct work for several years. It is easy to look back and see that this was a real blessing because it forced us to learn how to continue Paul's work while he was still there as a rock for us to lean on. His time in prison, first in Caesarea[51] and then in Rome,[52] meant that the work of direct preaching fell to others, and he became a sort of father figure to many of the congregations. A father they would listen to and learn from, but whom they couldn't meet without having to make a long trip. Quite a few believers chose to make that journey and benefitted greatly from Paul's wisdom. He never turned anyone away, and no-one was ever arrested by the Romans for visiting him either, though the frightening possibility was always there in the background.

After all those years in prison, Paul spent a final period of freedom preaching enthusiastically, before he was imprisoned once more and executed – but not before he had written some more valuable letters for us. Those of us who had been close to him felt very much alone. In some ways I think it must have been much how the disciples felt when Jesus was killed. Yet for us Jesus was still there, and the power of God was still with us to strengthen us in all that we did. But Paul had become much more of a father to me than my real father ever was, and I still miss him. He once told me that I shouldn't let

---

[51] Acts 24:26-27
[52] Acts 28:30-31

people despise my youth. Well, they can't do that now – I'm not young anymore! In fact, I don't expect to live much longer.

My life has been an incredible journey and I have seen some amazing changes in the world. I really have seen the world turned upside down.

It is fair to say that one man, Jesus Christ, started the process.

He showed that one man can change the lives of hundreds of thousands of people – possibly even more – simply by inspiration.

Many kings have changed the lives of millions before now, but they have done it through domination and intimidation, oppression and tyranny. Empires have ruled the world, but Jesus *led* the world, and now his followers have changed the world.

Just a few people drawn from many different walks of life – rich and poor, noblemen and commoners, soldiers and slaves. With the help of God, these few have overcome the world.

But the world is fighting back. It always does.

In one of his letters to me, Paul spoke of the false teachings of two false brothers as spreading like gangrene.[53] How right he was! I reminded them of our hope of resurrection, and did my best to charge them before God to keep this fundamental hope clear in their minds. I'm afraid that I have never found confrontation easy, even when it has to be faced up to, and I was probably not as blunt or uncompromising as Paul would

---

[53] 2 Timothy 2:16-18

have been. Maybe it wouldn't have made any difference, but anyway, they refused to listen to me.

Paul also warned that such people would lead others into more and more ungodliness. Well, they did, and I didn't seem to be able to stop it.

The world has fought back mostly through infiltration: quarrels about words and empty chatter have entered our fellowship as if we were just a group of ordinary people, not believers who are called to be like Jesus.

Towards the end of his life, even Paul had difficulty keeping some of the believers on the path of truth. Some were eager to gain positions of leadership, not because they wanted to lead God's people in faith, but because they liked authority and recognition from others. Paul could claim authority over them because of his selection by Jesus, but when Paul was killed, a lot of my confidence and authority died with him.

I knew the truth in detail: Paul taught me very thoroughly. But I had never seen Jesus, never heard his teaching, never been spoken to by him on the road to Damascus – and so when troublemakers came, I found it very hard to oppose them as resolutely as Paul had commanded me to. There was no doubt that God helped me, and that Jesus worked with his believers through me, but I feel that I let them down at times.

Following Jesus is an individual task in some ways, but as congregations we are meant to work together, and I fear that many of our congregations are now straying from the truth en masse – some through fear of the authorities, others through apathy or the leadership ambitions of men like Hymeneus and Philetus.

Already, some of the congregations that were flourishing in Paul's day no longer exist. I recently heard of a revelation made to John the apostle by Jesus that included letters to the seven congregations in Asia. Ephesus, a congregation dear to my heart for many years, is described as having lost their first love. He even threatens to remove their light completely unless they repent. Already they are condemned by our Lord Jesus, and only a change in attitude will rescue them.[54]

Other congregations are even worse, and sometimes I despair of what the future holds. Jesus once asked his disciples whether he would find faith in the earth when he returns.[55] I never took the question seriously while Paul was alive, but now it bothers me every day.

My time of service is coming to an end. The faith will slip from our grasp unless we revitalise our lives.

Come Lord Jesus – we need you.

---

[54] Revelation 2:5-6
[55] Luke 18:8

Twenty-Two

What to do?

For the true story, see 3 John.

"You did *what?*" thundered Diotrephes.

"I invited him into my house," I replied.

"But don't you know that he will just try to bring lies and division into our congregation?"

"But you haven't even met him," I protested.

"I don't need to. I've met people like him before," he sneered.

"We talked for hours yesterday evening, and he spoke nothing but truth."

"If that's what you think, Gaius, maybe we need to start checking on you!" The look on Diotrephes' face was threatening.

"Look, he brought a letter with him…"

"Don't they all? Letters from Paul, letters from Peter, letters from James – but they're all dead. Surely you understand! Nobody writes inspired letters any more: when people bring letters with them, they're frauds."

"But this was a letter from John, Diotrephes. The Apostle John, the disciple whom Jesus loved. The man who taught me the truth about God, and then baptised me."

"Oh, come on! He's much too old to be writing letters, and he's never been an author anyway. He only sends messengers, and I think he's probably going senile, based on the last few messages we've had from him. Remember that last man you invited into your house? There were plenty of people in the assembly who weren't happy with him and what he said. You didn't make yourself popular welcoming him."

"Of course I welcomed him. He came teaching truth and reminding us of Jesus' words of salvation. I learned a lot from him, and it would have helped lots of the brothers if you had allowed him to speak before the assembly."

"He was just coming to tell us what to do."

"Anyway," I continued, "we're not talking about him, we're talking about a letter, and this was a letter sent from John. It's written in his handwriting, too – I recognise it."

"Well, where is this letter then? Let me read what the old apostle John has to say to our congregation. Obviously he doesn't have any authority over us, but he just might have something worth reading."

"He didn't send it to our congregation. He sent it to *me*."

"I'm sorry, Gaius, but I think it must be a fraud. Even if John has taken up writing in his old age, he would hardly be likely to write to you, would he? He would write to the leaders in the assembly – people like me. I reckon your visitor wrote the letter himself, trying to make it look like John's writing."

"No, Diotrephes, the letter is genuine. And what he says makes sense too."

"If it makes sense, then it can't be from John. John's too old, and he's getting too carried away with his own importance. Just because he knew Jesus, he thinks we should all bow down to him and listen to everything he says. The fact is, he's almost illiterate, which is no real surprise – he was only a fisherman after all, and now he's too old even for that."

"Don't forget, he was one of the twelve that Jesus chose!"

"Yes, and so was Judas. The time of the apostles has passed. Jerusalem has been destroyed and the nation of Israel is no more. All the leaders amongst Jesus' followers are Gentiles now. The truth has moved on. If you need to know answers about God's word, come and ask me, don't listen to a crotchety old man."

"This 'crotchety old man', as you call him, is a messenger of the son of God. If you ignore him, you ignore God."

"You're living in the past, Gaius. The apostles are all dead and gone, except for senile old John. If John wants to send us messages, he should send them to me, then I can make sure that they're right."

"You'll have to tell him that yourself, Diotrephes. In fact, why don't you tell it to the messenger he sent? He's still at my home."

"He's still at your home? People like him are not welcome here, and if you insist on entertaining people like him, we'll have to review your membership of the assembly. Do you want to hang onto the past, welcoming people who just cause division? Gaius, it's coming to a point where you might have to make a choice. Do you want to be part of our dynamic group of believers in whom the word of God is growing and maturing?"

"Let's just stop here for a moment, Diotrephes. You said that John isn't a writer. Have you ever received a letter from him?"

"We all know that John doesn't write like Paul or any of the others." His look was evasive and so was his answer. This new letter from John had mentioned an earlier letter, and that convinced me to pursue the matter.

"Have you ever received a letter from John?" I persisted.

"Not personally."

"So you have received one that was not for you personally?"

"There was a short note a while ago."

"I don't remember that being mentioned in any of our meetings, Diotrephes. As one of the congregation, I would expect to hear about it."

"It wasn't important – it was all about John asserting his supposed authority. The congregation didn't need to hear it."

"So it wasn't a letter to you, but you stopped anyone from hearing about it?"

"That's a confrontational way of putting it, Gaius. You sound like Demetrius. Are you looking for a fight?"

"I'm just looking for truth, and I hope you are too. Do you know what John wrote to me about Demetrius?"

"Do I care? John's opinions are not very important here."

"John said, 'Demetrius has received a good testimony from everyone, and from the truth itself. We also add our testimony, and you know that our testimony is true.' Sounding like Demetrius could be a good thing, don't you think?"

"Well, I don't think he'll be getting a good testimony from this congregation for much longer. We've begun the process of expelling him for his stubborn refusal to accept the decisions of the elders. He persists in welcoming exactly the sort of so-called brothers you have staying with you now. I thought you were better than that, Gaius, but it seems that we may have to expel you too."

"Stop! Stop! Stop, Diotrephes! You are doing just exactly what he said about you!"

"Who?"

"John. He said that he had written a letter to the congregation, but that it had been rejected by you; then he said five things about you. Do you want to hear them?"

"No. He is trying to make himself the big boss. He has no authority here."

"That's what he said you were saying."

"Well, he keeps sending people who cause trouble. He should leave us alone. I and my friends are here to lead the congregation. He's just an old has-been, living in the past, back when Jerusalem and the temple were still around, when Peter and Paul and the rest were teaching. Not only that, but some of his memories of the past are just plain wrong anyway. He seems to forget that he and the other eleven didn't always get things right. Jesus didn't call James and John the 'Sons of Thunder' for nothing! And he is still too quick in calling for judgement on people who don't agree with him. We need to move with the times. And these times don't include John. These are our times where we…"

"He said that you would say things like that too!" I had heard enough, and interrupted without ceremony. "Why won't you listen to the words of a man whom Jesus loved enough to choose, first as one of his twelve disciples and then as one of the special three?"

"Gaius, you are a good brother, but you are being led away from the truth. If you don't start listening to us instead of trying to instruct us, we may have to discipline you too!"

"Diotrephes, I'm going to tell you what John said about you whether you want to hear it or not. There were five points he made about you: firstly, that you will not acknowledge his authority."

"Of course I will, but he shouldn't be trying to rule over everybody and keeping living in the past."

"His second point was that you like to put yourself first," I continued.

"That's ridiculous! I am a leader in the congregation because I was appointed to a position of leadership and have exercised it better than anyone else. If John would just stop trying to be the big boss over everyone, we wouldn't have these problems."

"Thirdly, he says that you speak wicked nonsense against him."

"Well, you know that one is completely false. Many, many times you've heard me praising John, but some of the men he sends to us are simply outside the bounds of godliness and fellowship. I hate to have to say it, but he's losing his grip, and we won't tolerate his stooges any more."

"Fourthly, he says that you refuse to welcome the brothers," I continued, smiling at the way his last words had so clearly proved John's charge.

"They're not our brothers, and if you want them as your brothers, then you won't be welcome either!" he shot back.

Despite the seriousness of the situation, I almost laughed, because all of his comments fitted so well with the very things John had condemned in him. "His fifth statement was that you put those who want to welcome the brothers out of the congregation – and that's just what you are threatening me with. Please, Diotrephes, listen to the Apostle's words. He wants unity and peace amongst the believers, but you're not going about things the right way."

Our discussion went on for a while, but Diotrephes was not in any mood to accept instruction. In parting, I asked him to stop and consider, while he threatened once more to exclude me from the congregation.

I went home and reread John's letter several times. How could our world-wide fellowship have come to this? Was not the church meant to be Jesus' body? One body? A body of unity and humility? I discussed the question with the brother who had delivered John's letter and we worried together. We continued our discussions the next day, concentrating on what the future of Jesus' church was, then the following day he left to return to John. He would not have a happy message to report. Maybe it would inspire John to visit us. I hoped so, but worried that it might already be too late.

The next day, I received a visit from Diotrephes, calling me to attend a meeting of what he called "The Elders" to answer certain accusations. Again I tried to reason with him, but he would have none of it and left with the words, "Just be there on Saturday night, Gaius. I'm warning you that if you won't listen to us, we'll have to count this discussion today as the start of the process of putting you out of the church – along with the rest of the troublemakers we've already got rid of."

The house is shaking[56]

After hearing that parting threat, I went immediately to see Demetrius. He welcomed me a little cautiously, I thought, and we spoke for a while on general matters before I brought up my reason for visiting. I told him about the letter John had sent and what he had said of Diotrephes, and of Demetrius himself. He was rather

---

[56] "Earthquake with house" by loveandread (OpenClipArt)
https://openclipart.org/detail/190876/earthquake-with-house

surprised to hear John's praise of himself, but pleased because it gave him more confidence that he was doing the right thing in opposing Diotrephes and his cronies.

"Did you know that I'm to be formally put out of the church tomorrow?" he asked sadly. "Gaius, what can we do? It is Jesus' congregation – what can I do if I can't be part of it?"

"I knew Diotrephes was working on it," I said, "but I didn't know it had got that far. I have an interview of my own with Diotrephes and his gang on Saturday. Obviously you made a better stand than I did – earlier, at least. I suppose they will throw me out, too."

"Is there anything we can do?"

"Maybe if John were to visit…"

"But he is very old. I'm sure he would like to come, but what if he can't?"

"Can it be that if the true believers are being put out of the church, the church is not Jesus' church anymore?"

"Maybe. We'll have to think about it. What are you doing on Sunday? I won't be welcome in the congregation any more."

"And after Saturday night, I probably won't be either," I responded, glumly. Neither of us was sure quite what it could all mean.

"If Diotrephes and those who follow him have taken over Jesus' church, what can we do? Are there enough people on the right side to be able to stop them?"

"I don't think so," I said slowly, mentally counting the few that I was confident about. "There are a few of us, but more of them."

"And all this has happened within only sixty years or so of Jesus going into heaven – and even while one of his chosen disciples is still alive. What a catastrophe!"

"And if this can happen in sixty years, how far will they be able to lead the church astray in a hundred years if Jesus doesn't come back before then?"

We stared at each other in consternation. Neither of us knew the answer, but we were both deeply worried.

Free Download

Paul in Snippets

An 81-page PDF novelette by Mark Morgan.

The life of Paul painted from the Acts of the Apostles.

Get your free copy of *Paul in Snippets* when you sign up for the Bible Tales mailing list. As well as the eBook, you will receive a weekly email newsletter with micro tales, informative articles and special offers.

Visit **http://www.BibleTales.online/free-pins**

www.BibleTales.online

Bible Tales Online

Other books by Mark Morgan are available from Bible Tales Online.

Terror on Every Side!

The Life of Jeremiah

From a family of priests in the peaceful reign of good King Josiah, came a young man Jeremiah, bringing words from God to his people. It was no message for the fainthearted, either. It was a message of *Terror on Every Side!*

Volume 1 – Early Days
Volume 2 – As Good As It Gets
Volume 3 – Darkness Falling
Volume 4 – The Darkness Deepens
Volume 5 – No Remedy (expected July 2019)

Generally available as paperback, eBook and audiobook.

Micro-tales

Collections of short stories about Bible characters or events, available in paperback, eBook and audiobook.
- ***Fiction Favours the Facts***
- ***Fiction Favours the Facts – Book 2***

Other novels

Joseph, Rachel's son

Joseph lived a privileged life in Canaan until his jealous brothers sold him into slavery in Egypt. There, the favourite son learned hardship and faced undeserved punishment.

Overcoming one trial after another, he finally faces the greatest test of all: power over his brothers

---

Bible Tales Online continues to publish books.
To find the list of currently available books, visit
http://www.BibleTales.online/books

www.BibleTales.online